The Crush Necklace

The Crush Necklace

Jessie Paddock

Scholastic Inc.

Copyright © 2019 by Jessie Paddock

ISBN 978-1-338-57103-5

10 9 8 7 6 5 4 3 2 1   19 20 21 22 23

Printed in the U.S.A.   40

First printing 2019

Book design by Yaffa Jaskoll

For my original crushes:
JP1, KS, AP, and 1990s ATL

It wasn't until Moni burst through the recreation center's double doors that tears finally exploded from her eyes. The night was quiet and the air thick, like a rotten milkshake. All she could hear was the faint bass of indistinguishable music coming from inside. And now, her own sobs, too, as Grace's words played on a loop in Moni's head:

Two weirdos who nobody even likes.

It started to drizzle.

Two hours earlier, Moni had hoped that her second Friday Night Skate would be an evening she wouldn't soon forget. Now, as the light rain turned to massive drops and her tears streamed from her eyes with almost equal ferocity, Moni wished she could erase everything about seventh grade.

She looked back at the royal blue doors behind her. Nobody had followed her outside. Not Johnny, and certainly not Grace. Moni thought back to the first time she had walked into that building with her neon windbreaker, acid-washed jeans, and specks of glitter twinkling around her indigo blue eyes. She thought about what she and Grace had discovered at the end of that night.

Moni shivered. Thunder rumbled overhead. The rain didn't stop.

She walked all the way home through the storm, neither avoiding nor searching for puddles. Her once-perky half ponytail sagged from the weight of the water, and her coarse denim jeans clung to her thighs. Though it was warm for October, her teeth chattered.

In her right hand was a necklace with a key-shaped charm—the cause of all this mess. She clutched it so tightly that the grooves on the key threatened to break the skin of her palm. The broken silver chain dangled through her fingers. The stone on the charm continued to churn and swirl, like a storm in the night.

By the time Moni arrived home, soaked to the bone and too tired to sob any longer, the stone became a flat, empty black.

But Moni had yet to notice.

Chapter One

Four weeks earlier . . .

"Grace, come here! You have to see this!" Moni shouted.

Usually, when Moni and Grace wandered into Tina's Treasures, it was just to browse. Or to kill time. Or to pretend they were high schoolers with simply nothing to do and absolutely nowhere better to be. Tina's Treasures was an enormous thrift store packed full with lots of junk and the occasional, well . . . treasure. But today Moni knew precisely what she was looking for. She was on a mission.

"Look!" Moni exclaimed, pulling a light pink jacket from a tightly packed rack of dusty outerwear.

"Um, the theme is 1990s, not 1990s grandma," Grace said, rolling her eyes.

"Yeah, but I could put some baby powder in my hair, and boom! Most original Friday Night Skate costume ever."

"You would not," Grace said, horrified. But Moni

and Grace, BFFs for five years and counting, knew that, yes, Moni probably would. There wasn't much Moni Hayes wouldn't do for a laugh.

"Okay, fine. Just keep your eyes peeled for something neon or something that reminds you of the Spice Girls, or the Verge," Moni said, naming two of her mom's favorite bands from high school. "We're going to do our first Friday Night Skate right."

"Duh," Grace reassured her.

When Grace suggested they go to the first Friday Night Skate of the school year—a monthly event held in the town's recreation center—Moni knew her costume had to be on point. And to twelve-year-old Moni, that meant dressing head-to-toe, no-detail-missed in something that screamed 1992 to 1996.

Though nobody could remember who made this rule, Friday Night Skate was strictly a seventh- and eighth-grade affair. Each month there was a different theme, and if there was one thing that Moni Hayes could easily get behind, it was a theme. Somehow, dressing in costumes always made Moni feel most like herself. Maybe that's what seventh grade (and the summer leading up to it, if you wanted to get technical about it) was missing: Costumes. Or themes. Or both.

The first week of seventh grade hadn't started out as Moni had expected. Not exactly. She assumed that it would be like a continuation of sixth grade, just like how fifth grade had been a continuation of fourth. But no: Seventh grade seemed to be undiscovered territory.

It certainly didn't help that, because of some sort of funding redistribution, the two middle schools in her district had been combined. Or rather, Mason Mill Middle School had absorbed Moni and Grace's old, totally reasonably sized middle school. As a result, Moni began seventh grade at a school that felt to be the size of a university. Moni was surrounded by what seemed like swarms of unfamiliar faces. So many of her new (and, now that she thought about it, old) classmates peered around the room for approval before they laughed at a joke. Moni constantly noticed groups of girls and boys whispering in the hallways, as opposed to speaking in normal voices. All in all, Moni was suddenly super aware of everything she and others said and did. Everyone and everything around Moni felt to be operating by a new set of rules. Moni was suddenly lost, and there was no instruction manual in sight.

Plus, thinking about this new boy—this curious Johnny Shim—made Moni's stomach churn. Churn in an unfamiliar but not entirely bad way. Ever since Moni had first noticed him that hot day outside of Bendy's, her favorite ice cream shop, a couple weeks back, her head had been prone to spinning and her stomach to churning. If seventh grade came with an instruction manual or a rule book, maybe all this spinning, churning, and overall jittery sensation could be explained.

But Moni had a feeling Johnny Shim was far too interesting to be explained in a rule book. Nobody who ordered Bendy's craziest ice cream flavor with such confidence could be explained in a rule book.

And now Moni was thinking about him. Yet again.

Moni took a deep breath to clear her head and persevered down aisle three, sneakers squeaking on the linoleum floor. Grace trailed her, more focused on the phone in her hand than the fashion all around her.

"This could work," Moni said, running her hand over a bedazzled jacket. "Kind of reminds me of a figure skating costume." Moni considered the jacket and compared it in her mind to the old photos of her mom that she'd consulted for outfit research.

"Don't you think that's a little . . ." Grace's voice trailed off.

"Jazzy?" Moni said, finishing her best friend's sentence, not missing the opportunity to wave her fingers in the air to emphasize her point.

"I was going to say *bright*, but sure."

"I don't see the problem."

"I can't pull that off, but you go for it," Grace said. "You really can rock any look."

"Nah. There's only one of these sparkly things, and we have to match."

"Good point."

"Anyway," Moni continued, "I'm partial to an acid-washed jean, neon windbreaker, scrunchie look, to be honest."

"Sure," Grace agreed.

Even though Grace didn't share Moni's instincts for theatrics, she was playful in her own way. She was always the first to laugh at a joke and was the kind of friend who would stay up all night chugging cherry Cokes or sneak outside at 3:00 a.m. to light sparklers left over from the Fourth of July. Grace was an excellent partner in crime and possessed the ability like no other to make Moni feel like she was at home, no matter their present location.

"Are you sure we're invited?" Moni asked with mock seriousness.

"Well, yes, I mean, we are seventh graders now. Plus, Harley texted me at lunch saying that it would be totally fun it we came."

Harley was Grace's new soccer friend, whom Grace couldn't stop talking about or texting with since their return from camp two weeks ago. Grace had her sights set on a college soccer scholarship, and when the most competitive girls' club in North Georgia, the Belleayre Fire, invited her to play with them at team camp, Grace jumped at the opportunity. This Harley girl was tall and outgoing and seemed to know everything about everything. At least that's what Grace said. Though Moni, Grace, and Harley were all students at the new and enormous Mason Mill Middle School, Moni had managed to avoid Harley for the entire first week of school.

"What if Harley's lying just to embarrass us?" Moni asked, only half-joking.

"Harley wouldn't lie, it's cool," Grace repeated, as if reassuring herself more than Moni.

"I'm kidding," Moni said, throwing her arm over her friend's shoulder. She hated it when Grace got that panicked look that had yet to fade from her face. It had been happening more and more recently, and it made her BFF seem far away somehow. "It's a free country; we don't need an invitation or approval."

For a split second, Moni hoped she was right about the approval part. She shook the thought out of her head almost as quickly as it had entered.

"Harley said we shouldn't get there before six thirty but definitely not after seven. I'll confirm right now." Grace's fingers whirred over the keypad on her phone, jotting down a text in what must have been world-record time.

"Right, right, fashionably late, I get it," Moni said as she sorted through some old leather jackets that were definitely too big, probably too expensive, and at the very least too mildewy.

It wasn't that Moni wasn't excited for Friday Night Skate. Quite the contrary. She'd been daydreaming about it for years. She had a picture in her mind: gliding across the polished gym floor, arm in arm with Grace, laughing at an inside joke nobody else knew, their favorite song of the moment playing in the background. That image was concrete in Moni's mind. Though plenty of seventh graders went, Moni had never imagined they'd dare go to Friday Night Skate before they were in eighth grade, when they were closer to the top of the middle school food chain, not at the beginning of seventh, where she still felt like a cod in a sea of sharks. Or a robin surrounded by owls and snakes. Or the one kid who forgot to wear a costume to the dress-up party. Four days into seventh grade, Moni felt more like a fish out of water than ever before. And it didn't help that Grace, buoyed by her new soccer friendships, seemed to be in the opposite boat.

Moni had noticed a certain shift in her BFF since she'd returned from soccer camp. Now, Grace spoke at a much quicker pace, she was glued to her phone, and whenever they went to any public place, her eyes kept darting around as if something exciting might come from around the corner at any minute. Moni didn't quite know what to make of it. Not yet. She was doing her best to keep up, even if she didn't always want to.

But Moni was determined to turn things around the next evening at Friday Night Skate. No matter what, she was going to have the time of her life with her cherry-Coke-and-mini-marshmallow-loving best friend. Period.

And no time like the present to start the shenanigans. The fact that "Dream Reality" by Heat Squad started playing over the store's crackly speakers was just plain good timing.

Heat Squad, Boys Jump, and the Verge songs were all staples in the Hayes household. Moni's mom said their tunes reminded her of prom, but in a good way. "Dream Reality," "Jaded 4 U," and "Palomino" were more than just vaguely cheesy love songs from her mom's past. To Moni, each song sounded like home; she knew all the lyrics by heart.

"You ready for this?" Moni asked, hiding between two racks of very ugly sweaters. She threw on the tackiest, most patterned, and largest sweater over her head and stepped into a rogue pair of gigantic plaid pants that were really best suited for a clown impersonator.

"Hello? Earth to Grace Lucia Diaz," she said when Grace didn't respond.

"One sec," Grace muttered, eyes still down in her phone. "Harley added me to a new group text with Raya and some of the strikers from the boys' team."

Another thing about Grace since soccer camp: She seemed to be on no fewer than five different group texts with this tall, outgoing, seemingly perfect Harley. Grace's phone was constantly buzzing. Moni still had a habit of leaving her phone at home, between couch cushions or even right there in plain sight on the kitchen counter. Grace was the only one who texted her anyway, and if Moni wasn't at home, she was probably with Grace.

By now the chorus was coming up, and Moni was unwilling to continue thinking about dumb group chats she wasn't on (and didn't want to be on, thank-you-very-much!) or continue waiting for Grace.

It was go time.

Moni burst out from behind the clothing rack, took a breath, and belted.

"I feel like I'm asleep! You're my dream reality! Don't know if I'm awake . . ."

If her eyes had been open, Moni would have seen that she almost knocked Grace's precious phone out of her hands. Or the look of half shock, half admiration on her best friend's face. But, perhaps most important, she would have noticed how far the base of the clothing rack extended, and it wouldn't have caught her toe.

But it had, and Moni plummeted to the floor, bringing at least a dozen hangers and ugly sweaters with her.

Still, Moni didn't stop singing as she fell.

"Don't you dare disappear!"

"I hate to say it, Moni, but I saw that coming a mile away," Grace said through bouts of hysterical laughter. Moni loved getting a good laugh from Grace; Grace's belly laugh was one of her very favorite sounds. "Please tell me you're okay?"

"You're my dream reality!"

Moni finished the hook somewhat feebly from the ground. She hated to let a song lyric go unfinished.

"I'm fine. Did anyone see?"

"Um, yeah, I think everyone saw. And heard," Grace said, slightly flushed. A few women with shopping carts full of housedresses peeked their heads over some overstuffed racks of collared shirts. Moni gave them her goofiest grin and two thumbs up.

"Eh, there are worse things." Moni popped back to her feet. "But don't try to tell me that the details on this epic sweater did not catch the beautiful fluorescent lights on my way down. It might be a keeper," Moni teased.

"Yes, I think I really saw its true colors." Grace

giggled, finally broken out of her text message haze. "Do you think people will actually be skating at this thing?"

"It's called Friday Night *Skate*, Grace," Moni pointed out. "Of course they will be."

"Maybe you should wear a helmet, then."

Moni smiled. "Probably not the worst idea."

"You are such a weirdo," Grace joked.

"Thank you kindly." Moni grinned. "Now help me pick up all these ridiculous sweaters."

Twenty minutes later, Moni found two oversized jazzy windbreakers and two pairs of high-waisted, acid-washed jean shorts. Now all she had to do was grab some scrunchies from the drugstore and they were in business.

"Let me guess," Roxanna, the cashier, said as they approached the register, "Friday Night Skate is nineties-themed this week." Roxanna had very tiny bangs, always chewed gum, wore too much eyeliner, and looked like she might be anywhere between sixteen and twenty-eight years old. Moni could never tell.

Moni and Grace nodded in unison.

"Rad, right?" Moni added.

"Sure. Rad," Roxanna said in the same disinterested tone.

Moni placed her findings on the counter while Grace tried on sunglasses from a rack behind them. Moni heard Grace's phone ping, indicating yet another incoming text.

"Ooh! Harley says we should roll with them to Friday Night Skate tomorrow!"

Moni felt her stomach flip and then shrink to the size of an acorn.

"Like forward roll?" she asked, trying to joke her way out of what felt like a dense fog rapidly descending over her mood.

"Har-har," Grace said, rolling her eyes. "I think they're coming from Harley's, so I'll tell them to just meet us at your place since it's on the way and we can walk the rest of the way together!"

"Who's *they*?"

"Raya, for sure, and maybe someone else from the team. It will be so fun to go in one big group!"

"*So* fun," Moni murmured sarcastically, not quite loud enough for Grace to hear. She felt as if something essential had just been taken from her.

Stop being dramatic, Moni thought. *You're still*

going with Grace. There will just be a few more people there. It's not that different than you imagined.

Moni swallowed. In an effort to escape her thoughts, she focused her attention on the presentation of trinkets by the register.

And it was then that Moni saw the necklace. There, on display, perched inside a red velvet box beneath the glass countertop. Moni didn't feel so much like she was the one looking at the necklace, but rather the necklace was peering at *her.*

It was actually the charm that caught her eye first: a small silver key, with a dark blue stone at the top. Nothing about the key was fancy, but Moni couldn't take her eyes off that small circular stone. It was a shade of blue she'd never quite seen before, a bit darker than navy and deeper than a moonless night. It reminded her of putting her ear to a seashell and hearing the ocean: infinite, absorbing, and mysterious. Moni didn't wear a lot of jewelry, but she realized that, without question, she wanted to put on that necklace and maybe never take it off.

"Whoa," Moni said without thinking.

"*Whoa* yourself," Roxanna mocked. She was not hired for her customer service.

"How much is that necklace?" Moni had fifteen dollars left after her shopping spree. She didn't want to spend all of it today, but if she had to in order to get the necklace, she would.

"That old thing?" Roxanna pulled it out from inside the display and searched the back of the box for a price tag. "We've had this since basically forever. It's supposed to be like a mood ring, but I think it's broken."

Weird. Moni had been a regular patron of Tina's Treasures since basically forever and she'd never noticed the necklace before. She wondered why today of all days the remarkable charm had suddenly caught her eye.

"What's a mood ring?" Moni asked.

Roxanna rolled her eyes.

"Kids," she muttered under her breath. "A mood ring is a ring, obviously, with a stone that changes colors depending on your mood. For example"—Roxanna held the necklace up to her collar—"if it worked, it would change to a different color to clearly indicate that I'd rather be on my couch eating a Hawaiian pizza and playing video games instead of selling broken necklaces to fourth graders."

"Seventh graders, actually," Grace corrected her from behind a pair of mirrored frames.

"Exactly," Roxanna said. "This baby will cost you seven bones—no more, no less."

"I'll give you five dollars for it," Moni interjected. She was no stranger to bargaining with Roxanna.

"Sold."

Moni grabbed the necklace from Roxanna's hands, quickly clasping it around her neck, in case Roxanna changed her mind. Moni had the feeling that the necklace, or at least the charm, was worth much more than five measly dollars.

"That stone is the same color as your eyes," Grace said, looking at Moni over a pair of gigantic red frames.

Moni batted her eyelashes. Moni's eyes were her favorite feature, mainly because they matched her mom's.

"How amazing," Roxanna said, still unimpressed.

"What about these sunglasses?" Grace asked, throwing on a pair of Wayfarers with reflective lenses. "They're kinda the perfect thing to finish off our outfits, right?" She already had her phone out, camera app pulled up, prepped for a selfie.

"They sure are," Moni said, grabbing the sunglasses off Grace and placing them over her own eyes. "Were they made for my face or what?" Moni asked jokingly, sticking out her tongue and throwing up a peace sign for good measure.

Grace held up her phone for the selfie. But the moment Moni saw their reflection on the screen, her face froze and her stomach flipped.

There he was, head as much framed in the photo as theirs.

Johnny Shim.

Standing within touching distance right behind them.

Moni swiveled around to face him, because how could she not? She had never been this close to Johnny Shim before. At least not to his face. To keep herself steady, she started counting the freckles on his nose. *One . . . two . . . three . . . four . . .*

"Yes. Made for Moni Hayes and nobody else," Johnny said.

Moni hadn't realized he knew her last name.

Five . . . six . . . seven . . . eight . . .

Johnny smiled. He had a dimple on his left cheek.

Moni's knees almost buckled as Grace kicked her

from behind—her cue to speak. Moni had no idea how long she had actually been counting freckles.

"Uh—you too!" Moni squeaked.

Johnny looked at her quizzically but then smiled again, even bigger this time. Moni thought she heard Grace mutter "OMG" as she exhaled.

"Skate should be fun," Johnny said, handing Roxanna a ten-dollar bill. "I'll see you both there?" He threw a fairly gigantic green-gray-and-white flannel shirt over his shoulder and walked out the front door.

Before Moni and Grace had a chance to react, Roxanna jumped in.

"Nope, I've never seen that thing change colors," Roxanna said, gesturing to Moni's necklace.

Moni looked down at the charm. Sure enough, the circular stone suddenly glowed a bright blue.

"You must have powers beyond your control," Roxanna added in a way that immediately made Moni nervous. "Your treasure, or Crush Necklace, comes with this box, free of charge."

"Crush what?" Moni squeaked. How did Roxanna know? What was she accusing Moni of? Where did this talk of crushes suddenly come from?! "I didn't say anything about crushes!" Moni's cheeks tingled and her heartbeat increased to the point where she could feel her pulse pounding behind her eardrums.

"Um, I know, I have ears," Roxanna said, pointing to a white sticker on the bottom of the box. There, in faded, handwritten print, someone had scrolled *Crush Necklace* in a wobbly cursive. "This fancy red case is probably worth more than that old necklace."

"Huh," Grace said. Moni had nearly forgotten Grace was by her side. Without looking at her best friend, Moni knew she had that trademark mischievous twinkle in her eye. "What a coincidence."

"Now pay and get out of here," Roxanna barked. "I'm about to go on break."

"I knew it! You have a crush on Johnny Shim!" Grace exclaimed once they were in the parking lot. The humid air was not as refreshing as Moni had hoped. It was going to rain.

"What do you mean? How?"

"Um, well, in case you have amnesia, you've been talking about him nonstop ever since I got back from camp."

There was a chance that Grace was right. Sure,

she had mentioned the ice cream, the rocks, and the run-in at the deli. And then there was the second day of school. She'd bragged to Grace that everybody at lunch, including "that new guy, Johnny Shim, who's kind of nice and maybe cute or whatever," thought the face mask she'd made out of salami was hilarious.

Okay, fine. Maybe Moni had talked about him a little.

Or a lot.

So what?

It's not like she wanted to talk about him, or think about him, even. She couldn't help it. He was always just right there circling her brain. And it seemed there was absolutely nothing she could do about it. In fact, Moni only sort of knew Johnny Shim at all because Grace had abandoned her for a whole week to go to soccer camp. This was all Grace's doing!

"I personally think y'all are perfect for each other," Grace said as the girls walked the short mile back to the apartment Moni shared with her mom.

"Really?" Moni asked, giving away more excitement than she had meant to. "Why? I mean, I don't disagree, but did you pick up on something?"

"Just a feeling I get. Similar vibes," Grace confirmed. Grace was getting wiser with age, Moni thought. "OMG, this is going to be so fun! Moni's first major crush!"

Moni didn't know if she should be embarrassed or proud.

"He's going to ask you to skate with him tonight, I just know it!"

"What if he doesn't, though? Could I ask him?"

"Sure," Grace answered, sounding unconvinced.

"Anyway, I'm not sure if he even likes me. He is very hard to read. Let's not talk about it," Moni said as much to herself as to Grace. "We've been looking forward to Friday Night Skate for literally years. All I want to do is boogie my butt off with you."

Just then, the clouds above them crashed together and the skies unleashed. Rain poured down.

"Run!" Moni screamed.

As the girls sprinted through the warm September rain, Moni made sure to splash in every puddle. For good luck, and for fun, and because getting caught in rainstorms and splashing in puddles was something that they'd been doing since they were little kids, and was something Moni planned to continue doing forever.

Chapter two

Johnny Shim truly was the kind of kid that was hard not to think about. Not once you'd met him. And as Moni was starting to learn, thinking sometimes translated to talking.

The first time Moni saw Johnny Shim, she was sitting on a picnic table outside of Bendy's, eating an ice cream cone. Moni remembered being very sweaty and the cone very drippy, but she was so groggy from the heat that she just let the rivers of melted mint chip cascade down the side of the sugar cone and over her hand. She was happy, hot, and enjoying the early symptoms of a sugar rush, when she noticed a boy about her age saunter through the seating area toward the counter. She'd watched with curiosity as he ordered. He wore purple high-top Converse, and his hair reminded her of a cumulous cloud. He paid in exact change and then walked right by her and down the street, eating a scoop of starry night out of a cup. Moni had been a regular at Bendy's for years and she'd never seen anyone over the age of six order that flavor before. First it turned your lips blue and then green, for some reason. Johnny Shim's lips were already a lizardy emerald by the time he walked by, but he didn't seem to notice. Or care.

Moni spoke to Johnny a couple days later, when she found him painting by the lakeshore. He had a pile of rocks, each one no bigger than a peanut butter cup, on his right and a piece of tinfoil covered in globs of multicolored paint to his left.

She went right up to him and asked, "What are you doing?"

"Making scenes," he answered without lifting his head.

For a minute, she watched him.

"This is the beginning of my dream from last night," he explained as he carefully brushed yellow swirls on a flat piece of slate.

"Those are little rocks. Little for painting, I mean."

"I find little rocks are the best for big dreams."

Moni thought about that for a while.

"Something from nothing," she finally said, though she didn't know why. "I'm Moni."

He continued to paint.

She wanted to watch him until he finished painting his dream. She actually wanted to watch him paint all afternoon, but she got the impression he didn't like an audience.

No, he didn't *need* an audience.

Johnny finally introduced himself at the minimart the next day. Moni was in aisle two, deciding between tennis racket–shaped pasta and elbows for their special Thursday night dinner.

"By the way," he said, coming straight to her as if they'd been in mid-conversation. "I'm Johnny Shim."

"Nice to meet you," Moni said, because she had good manners.

He explained that he had just moved to town from Portland in Maine (not Portland in Oregon) with his mom and dad and older brother, who had gotten kicked out of high school again and his mom just couldn't take it anymore so this was where they landed. That day he'd been wearing an old T-shirt with a picture of the universe and an arrow pointing to the center with the phrase *You are here.*

I am right here, Moni thought as she walked home, elbow pasta shaking like a tired maraca in her bag.

She saw him around a few more times after Grace returned. Sometimes they said hello and exchanged a few words. Now that school had started, she saw some form of him every day, even if it was only a wisp of his cloud hair or the tip of a purple sneaker.

Moni had never met anyone quite like Johnny Shim, and now it was obvious that she couldn't stop thinking and apparently talking about him.

She felt a little silly for not realizing her feelings earlier. Why else was she always looking out for his silhouette when she walked into the drugstore for a bag of chips or down the halls at school? Why else would she be in an unusually foul mood if he didn't say hello when they passed each other after math class, but felt like she was on top of the world when he laughed at her lunch-meat sheet mask goof? How come she hoped he admired her messy ponytail in gym class, or pictured how she could impress him by catching a small candy tossed from a distance into her mouth?

This crush on Johnny Shim was very complicated.

That evening, after she'd said goodbye to Grace and taken a long, hot shower, Moni sat at the kitchen counter, sipping on a tall glass of iced tea, while her mom made dinner. Thursdays they always had what Moni's mom called *disposal dinners*: every vegetable left in the fridge over pasta plus a lot of Parmesan cheese.

"Where's your mind at, Love Straw?" Moni's mom asked. She'd started referring to Moni as Love Straw when she was still pregnant ("Hormones are a crazy thing," she'd say whenever asked about the nickname's origin), and it just stuck. She even had a little graphic of two old-fashioned-looking straws linked together by a red heart tattooed on the side of her calf.

"Just school stuff. Nothing crazy," Moni fibbed.

Moni and her mom had moved 120 miles north from Atlanta to the not-too-tiny but definitely not-too-big lakeside town of Mason Mill five years ago. Neither of them missed the city. The day they signed the lease on their first apartment, Moni's mom went out and got a tattoo on the belly of her forearm that said *Be yourself. Everyone else is taken.* with a flower next to it. It was written in delicate cursive, and Moni still liked to trace the letters with her fingertip when they watched TV together, or when her mom fell asleep in the middle of one of her online business classes.

"Are you excited about the big Friday Night Skate tomorrow?" Moni's mom asked as she dumped the remains from two different pasta boxes into a pot of boiling water.

"Yes, I think so."

"You think?"

"No, I'm pretty sure I am," Moni corrected herself. "I found these amazing windbreaker jacket zip-up things that you can probably see from outer space. And I'm pretty sure I can make the acid-washed jeans we found even more acidy, like the ones you wore in that yearbook picture." If Moni was being honest, her mom's sixteen-year-old self inspired their entire look. "So that will be cool."

"Jazzy jackets. Love it. Great look for you girls," Moni's mom assured her.

"We're going with Grace's new soccer friends."

Moni liked to tell her mom everything, and she knew enough to know that meant she had a very special mom. Grace talked to Mrs. Diaz about next to nothing. "From what I hear they're very knowledgeable. And tall."

"You like 'em?"

"I don't really know them yet."

Moni's mom tested the pasta. Half elbows, half tennis rackets. Moni had never played tennis. It looked sort of fun. Did Johnny Shim like tennis? Moni pictured him swinging a life-sized racket made out of pasta instead of whatever real rackets were made out of. The image caused her to smile uncontrollably.

Moni took a sip of iced tea. Her mom always had a pitcher of semisweet hibiscus ready in the fridge. The fuchsia color was as wonderful as the tea itself.

"Three minutes left on the pasta, I'd say," her mom said. "Which means we got just enough time for our fun facts. Give it to me, baby girl."

Moni smiled. Fun fact time was Moni's favorite tradition. At the end of every day (or beginning, if Moni's mom had a late shift at the diner), they exchanged a fun fact. Sometimes it was an actual fact that one had learned, sometimes it was an observation, and sometimes it was just a feeling or a word. Often it was a moment in their day that stood out for one reason or another above the rest. But most important, a fun fact was always a fact—it was always true.

Moni had started officially recording her fun facts in a small red notebook she'd received for her birthday the year before. "For important things," her mom had said when she'd handed her the gift, wrapped carefully in newspaper. It was one of Moni's most prized possessions; she'd even put a strip of masking tape across the cover that read *TOP SECRET (JUST KIDDING) (OR AM I???)* in big block letters. From that point on, Moni documented all her fun facts in that notebook. Though she didn't tell anyone this—not Grace, not even her mom—Moni thought the notebook could serve as a time capsule, a way for her to remember bits of her life that might have otherwise been forgotten or overlooked. For that reason, she recorded her fun facts with scientific precision. Because precision was very important, as Moni wanted to be a scientist of some sort. Or artist slash costume designer. She'd yet to make up her mind. Either way, Moni's fun fact journal was something she kept just for herself.

"You first," Moni said. She wasn't sure what

direction to go in yet. Recently all that thinking and talking about Johnny Shim had also translated into many a Shim-themed fun fact. He had taken up a lot of real estate in her fun fact journal. She'd recorded their first three interactions in her best handwriting.

Fun Fact #84: Purple Converse complement a starry night mouth, she'd written when she'd returned home from Bendy's.

Fun Fact #85: Tiny rocks are the best for big dreams. That was one of the best fun facts of the whole summer.

Fun Fact #86: You are here. Simple, but Moni thought it was very profound.

"Let's see. I'm going to give you a good one," Moni's mom said, her slight Southern accent slipping out. She roughly chopped some not-so-fresh broccoli in silence for a moment. "Bananas contain a natural chemical that makes people feel happy."

"Really?"

"According to my regular Charlie. After he told me, he proceeded to order a half stack of blueberry, not banana, which I thought was pretty funny."

Moni chuckled, and her mom continued to chop.

"Your turn. No more thinking!" Moni's mom said once all the broccoli was in bite-sized pieces.

"Johnny Shim has more freckles than I can count."

Moni didn't expect that to be the fun fact that popped out. She hadn't even written it down in her book yet. There were probably—actually, definitely—a lot of people out there who had more freckles than she could count.

"An infinite freckle count is no small accomplishment," Moni's mom said with a slight grin. "This Johnny Shim sounds most impressive."

"He is," Moni said, again without thinking.

Moni's mom grabbed a jumbo-sized carton of Parmesan from the fridge while Moni considered all the ways Johnny Shim had already proven to be impressive.

"That's a pretty necklace you got there," Moni's mom said, looking up. "Tina's is finally selling an actual treasure or two."

Moni looked down at her necklace.

"I think it's good luck," Moni said with a grin.

After dinner and an episode of Moni and her mom's favorite reality show about couples who buy private islands in the Caribbean, Moni lay in bed and twirled the charm of her new necklace around her fingers. She thought about what Grace had said.

You have a crush on Johnny Shim.

Grace was most definitely right.

That night Moni dreamed of swirls, skates, and freckles.

Chapter Three

"Say 'Boo-ya!'"

"Boo-ya!" Moni screamed, striking her most dramatic pose, which at that moment meant shooting both hands high in the air and balancing on one leg with her foot propped up on her inner knee in a modified tree pose. Grace stood next to her, one hand on her hip, smiling, while Moni's mom snapped a burst of photos on her phone.

Any innocent person driving by the parking lot of Moni's apartment complex would have thought it was Halloween. That's how good Moni's and Grace's costumes were. Moni had worked her magic and transformed your average acid-washed thrift find into positively vintage denim wonders. Their purple-pink-and-green-zigzagged jackets doubled as reflective vests, they were so bright. Moni's mom had even surprised the girls with matching chokers made of simple black ribbon. The girls each wore oversized scrunchies, Grace's straight licorice-colored hair in a French braid down her back, bangs teased to perfection, and Moni's wavy auburn locks tied into a perky half ponytail. Grace added tiny dabs of glitter gel to their eyelids and cheekbones (unclear if glitter was officially a 1990s thing, but Moni had to admit it was a nice touch, so she let it slide). Their Wayfarer sunglasses topped off the look.

"One more for me," Moni's mom insisted.

"Mom, we have a gazillion already," Moni complained, though without needing additional encouragement she and Grace threw their arms around each other instinctually, just as they had for so many photos over the past five years.

Grace's phone made a *ding*. "Harley and them will be here in just a sec," Grace said.

Moni forced a smile. Harley and them—*them* being Raya—were late. Moni was anxious to get to the rec center already.

"Thanks for taking the pics, Nikki," Grace said. Moni's mom insisted that Grace call her by her first name. "I'm not that old yet!" she liked to say when anyone called her Mrs. Hayes. "Moni, let's take a selfie real quick."

Grace stretched her phone out in front of them, trying a few different expressions before settling on one and taking the picture. Moni stuck out her tongue and pretended to pick her nose.

"Gross, Moni! C'mon, just do one normal one."

"Fine." Moni popped on her shades and gave a deadpan stare into the camera while Grace pursed her lips and pretended to kiss someone or something that wasn't there.

Moni did not love taking serious selfies.

Correction: Moni did not love taking serious selfies where she could see herself as the picture was being taken. Selfies on old-fashioned cameras like the weird disposable one she found in her mom's purse once were all right.

A few minutes and what felt like a gazillion selfies later, Moni heard an unfamiliar voice coming from the end of the parking lot.

"G-Money!"

Moni turned and saw a girl wearing cutoff shorts and a white tank top with *Sporty Spice* drawn on the front with a permanent marker. Harley. The other girl by her side, Raya, by default, wasn't even pretending to be in a costume. Both Harley and Raya were very tall and very pretty. Glamorous, maybe, despite their lack of costumes.

"Harley!" Grace exclaimed.

Grace and Harley exchanged another hug before Grace officially introduced Moni to her new soccer friends.

"Harley plays center back, and Raya is center mid," Grace explained to Moni, as if the difference between the two positions was both significant and obvious.

"And our girl Grace, the next best winger to happen to Belleayre Fire since basically ever!" Harley complimented, giving Grace a high five.

"Wait, you officially made the team? You didn't tell me that!" Moni exclaimed.

"Yeah, I mean nothing is set in stone or anything," Grace said, playing down the accomplishment.

"That's so awesome!" Moni nearly tackled Grace with a hug. Moni knew what a big deal this was for Grace, and honestly was a little surprised she hadn't told her immediately.

"So aggressive, Moni. No need to tackle me," Grace said, shrugging Moni off.

"Oops." Moni took a step back.

"Anyway, you guys are totally decked out!" Harley said. "So cute!"

"Festive," Raya added. Raya spoke in a way that made it seem like she might not actually have enough air in her lungs to get the whole word, much less a sentence, out.

"No costumes for y'all?" Moni asked. She couldn't imagine going to a costume party without a costume. That would be like eating a peanut butter sandwich without the jelly. French fries without ketchup *and* ranch dressing. Summer without fireworks!

"We decided to go *au naturel*," Raya explained, using an accent at the end that she probably thought sounded French. Moni wasn't convinced.

"Y'all look amazing!" Moni's mom said. "Call me if you need a ride home. I switched shifts so I'll be in all night studying. Big Friday for Nikki Hayes, ladies and gentlemen."

"Thanks, Mom, we'll be fine," Moni said. "It's only like a ten-minute walk."

"Okay, love you, have fun, don't do anything I

would or wouldn't do, skate your li'l hearts out, and I'll see you at nine thirty!"

"Your mom's, like, cool," Harley said once they'd left the parking lot.

"Yeah, I know," Moni answered.

"What does that tattoo say?" Harley continued, gesturing to the soft spot on her forearm. "I couldn't quite read it. I didn't want to be rude and, like, stare, you know."

"Um, I don't remember the exact wording," Moni lied. She didn't want to share that special part of her mom with this tall, pretty, maybe sort of nice girl she'd just officially met.

As the group of four continued toward Friday Night Skate, Harley and Raya, who both had older siblings in high school, wasted no time telling Moni and Grace about the night ahead.

"So BG, Much Love, and Easy will probably take command of the stage," Raya predicted.

"We know them from soccer camp," Grace whispered to Moni.

"Is it a requirement that boys from soccer camp

have completely ridiculous names?" Moni asked nobody in particular.

Raya ignored Moni's question.

"Before I forget, lake tomorrow?" Harley asked. "It's supposed to be the last super-hot day."

"Long live summer!" Raya declared.

"Fun!" Grace said.

Fun? Moni thought.

"Anyway," Raya said, getting back on track. She was all business. "The stage is the place to be," she noted.

"If you're not skating with someone," Harley added.

"You always have to skate with someone. Nobody skates alone. That would be weird."

"Insane," Harley confirmed.

"Duh."

"Duh."

Raya and Harley were quite the tag team.

"There's a stage?" Moni finally asked. Raya and Harley's banter was starting to make her brain hurt.

"Yeah, obviously. Right behind the far side of the court, or rink, or whatever," Raya retorted.

"Think of it as a long bench," Harley said somewhat gently.

"Totally," Grace chimed in.

"Okay," Moni said.

After a couple minutes more of Raya talking about how the snack bar worked (didn't seem that complicated), Harley emphasizing that all the skates tended to be a size too large (good to know), and Grace agreeing with everything they said (annoying), Grace and Harley broke off a few paces ahead, presumably to talk about being above-average soccer players. Moni walked a few steps behind with Raya.

"I bet BG is going to ask Sophie out," Raya said. "We thought he liked V-Dawg, but that was before the whole lunch-box controversy."

Moni couldn't help but release a laugh. Raya shot her a look.

"Sorry," Moni muttered. "I'm just trying to imagine how a lunch box could be controversial. Like it wasn't big enough? It smelled like eggs? It didn't come with a thermos?" Moni giggled at her own joke.

"Oh, it was a con-tro-ver-sy," Raya responded, not sounding particularly amused.

"Anyway," Harley said, turning to Moni. "Grace says you have yourself a crush!"

Moni snapped her gaze to Grace, who shrugged sheepishly. She mouthed the word *sorry*.

"Wait, did you skip a grade?" Raya asked Moni suddenly.

"What? No. Why do you think I— Do I look young or something?" Moni answered, a bit flustered.

"Maybe it's the costume," Raya said with a shrug.

Moni glanced down at her outfit. She touched the glitter on her cheeks to make sure it was still there, before realizing that touching it might rub it off. She didn't look young. She looked like a teenager circa 1994 . . . right?

"OMG, you're ridiculous," Harley said, swatting at Raya. Raya shrugged and pulled her phone from her back pocket.

"I didn't skip a grade. I'm a normal seventh grader," Moni said. And then again, for emphasis, "A totally normal seventh grader. And yes, I have a crush on this new boy, actually."

Something about having a crush on a boy who was from a totally different state made the whole thing feel sophisticated in a way she hadn't yet considered.

"That's so fun!" Harley said. "Friday Night Skate is, like, the best place to get your crush on. You might even be able to sneak a kiss," she added with a wink.

"Nice," Grace said.

"O . . . kay." Moni was too preoccupied wondering what she'd even say to Johnny Shim. Kissing seemed out of the question to her.

"He doesn't know you like him yet, does he?" Raya asked.

"I don't know." Something else Moni had yet to consider.

"Good. You kind of want him to know you like him, but don't tell him or anything." Raya shivered. "That would be nuts. Just play it cool. If he likes you, he'll come to you. Duh."

"Duh," Harley echoed. "And don't worry if you don't get a spot on the stage. He might still ask you to skate anyway."

"Just play it cool," Harley repeated.

Moni took a deep breath. All these instructions were really starting to stress her out.

Chapter four

When the girls arrived at precisely 6:42 p.m., Friday Night Skate was already in full swing.

Harley and Raya immediately ran off to hug and shriek with some boys Moni didn't recognize. Soccer camp boys, Grace confirmed. Grace and Moni stood by the entrance for a moment, taking it all in.

The snack bar (a foldout table selling one-dollar sodas, chips, and candy) was stocked, and DJ 10 Foot, a tenth grader with matchstick arms, crouched self-importantly over a stickered laptop in the corner. The skate floor, more precisely a basketball court flanked by splintery wooden bleachers, lit by haloed fluorescents and a tired disco ball, was dusty and smelled slightly of mothballs, but was otherwise perfect. It was everything Moni expected, except . . .

"Nobody is wearing a costume," Moni whispered to Grace.

That wasn't exactly true. Nobody was wearing an *entire* costume. Maybe Raya and Harley weren't going to feel out of place in their looks after all. Most kids Moni saw had one clothing item that implied 1990s—a flannel here, a fanny pack there—but nobody was decked out head to toe.

Nobody except for Moni and Grace.

"Yeah, and nobody is skating."

"But everyone is wearing skates," Moni noted, still undeterred. "So come on. Let's lace up!"

"Okay, lemme get a pic of you in the disco ball lights real quick," Grace said, phone already teed up.

"Fiiiine," Moni agreed, mostly because she was so proud of her outfit. She pointed one finger in the air and placed her other hand on her cocked hip.

"Photo bomb!" Moni heard a scratchy voice from behind her yell as the flash of the photo went off. She turned and found Alex laughing.

Alex was the worst. He'd been making fun of Moni since second grade. When they were eight, he stole her sneaker right off her foot and hid it in a closet. Since fourth grade, he sporadically accused her of cheating for no reason when they played dodgeball in gym class. Alex smelled like applesauce and con-stantly had popcorn stuck in his braces.

"Going all in with the costume, I see," he smirked.

"Get out of here, jerk!" Grace yelled back. But Alex had already wandered off, probably to make dumb fart jokes with his dumb friends. "You're horrible!" she added for good measure.

"Ugh, I hate him," Moni said. "He's always so rude."

"Whatever, you look great."

"*We* look great!" Moni insisted. She hoped she was right. "C'mon, let's go."

The girls walked to the nearby converted custo-dial closet. They both traded their sneakers for size-five skates and moved to the nearest open bench to put them on.

And then, just as Moni finished lacing up her skates, Johnny Shim walked in with a group of boys. Moni's throat suddenly felt dry, so she tried to make eye con-tact with Johnny. But he walked right past Moni and Grace without so much as a nod.

"I don't get it," Moni said, watching Johnny. "He seemed so pumped yesterday at Tina's, and now he's not even giving me the time of day."

"Maybe you should ignore him," Grace suggested.

"Would he even notice? Also, why would I do that if I want hang out with him?"

"Harley says playing hard to get always works."

"Pshh." Something told Moni that Johnny Shim was nothing like the guys that Harley knew.

"This would all be so much easier if I could just read his mind!" Moni exclaimed.

"Duh," Grace agreed, blotting her lips on a tissue.

An hour later, most of the kids had broken into clumps of fours or fives scattered around the perimeter of the gym. Moni and Grace found a new bleacher spot to perch on while they shared a cup of pretzels. Moni didn't see Johnny anywhere. A growing crowd of kids that may or may not have included Harley and Raya gathered around the entrance to the stairwell. A girl with a lot of glitter on her face seemed to be making an announcement. Grace sat, oblivious, swiping through pictures on her phone, and Moni fidgeted with the key charm on her necklace. She liked the way the grooves of the key and the smooth surface of the stone felt on her fingertips. There was something comforting about the contrasting textures.

"Alex's braces look kind of like a diamond grill because of the flash in this picture," Grace said.

"He wishes," Moni said.

"True."

"I hate to say it, but Friday Night Skate is kind of a bust," Moni said glumly.

"I think Johnny might have left," Grace said without looking up.

"I don't even mean him," Moni said. "Yeah, he's being super annoying and whatever, but it doesn't seem like anyone is having any fun. Literally nobody is skating!"

Moni let out a sigh she didn't realize she'd been holding. She was ready to go home.

"Last song of the night!" DJ 10 Foot's voice announced over the crackly PA system. "Friday Night Skate will be back the first Friday of next month. But in the meantime . . ." The voice trailed off as the unmistakable intro to a very familiar tune began.

"Pinch me, I know I'm dreaming . . ."

Moni jumped to her feet, nearly slipping on her skates again.

"I don't know what is real . . ."

"We have to!" she cried.

Grace giggled and looked around. Nobody else seemed excited. Yet.

"We can't be the only ones skating," she said shyly, although Moni suspected that the part of Grace that Moni loved most—her mischievous, daring quality that had been hidden more often than not in the post–soccer camp weeks definitely thought they could be.

So Moni did what felt like the only obvious choice: She serenaded Grace.

"I feel like I'm asleep!"

Moni grabbed both of Grace's hands in hers, clutching them to her chest.

"You're my dream reality!"

Then Moni pretended to faint, lying out right there on the ground. By the next lyric, she was on her knees.

"It must be midnight! You're my dream reality!"

Moni launched herself into the middle of the floor, arms wide, gliding on one leg like someone who had no idea how much it would hurt if she came crashing down on the wooden floor. But even if she had known, she wouldn't have stopped. She had the entire skate floor to herself, and she wasn't going to waste it. Now she not only had Grace's attention, but several groups watched her increasingly epic performance.

Moni really did love an audience.

She proceeded to take a lap around the floor, windbreaker and half ponytail billowing behind her. Moni did a round of the Macarena (thank you, YouTube), then invented some moves of her own, at one point even trying a 360-degree turn. When she returned to Grace, who was still seated at their spot on the bleachers, laughing and cheering her on, Moni grabbed her hands and pulled her to her feet. To her slight surprise, Grace didn't resist.

And then something amazing happened: Others joined in. By the second chorus, almost everyone was on the floor, moving in a clockwise loop. Moni and Grace skated next to each other, hand in hand, just like she had always imagined.

When the long instrumental portion of the song started, Moni turned to Grace and cried, "This is so fun!"

But before Grace could respond, Harley whizzed up to Grace's other side.

"Slingshot time!" she yelled. "Come on!" And without giving Grace an option, or Moni time to protest, she pulled Grace forward. Moni tried to hold on, but their hands slipped apart.

Moni wasn't one to be easily defeated or left out, not when her veins surged with this much adrenaline. If they were going to slingshot or whatever, Moni would just slingshot with them.

She dug her right skate into the floor for a burst of speed, but she must have caught a patch of dust or a ridge in the old wooden planks, and instead of gliding smoothly up to Grace's side, she Supermanned across the floor and into the bleachers.

All things considered, it was a spectacular fall.

Moni slid and slid, only coming to a stop in front of a pair of skates with purple-and-red-polka-dotted socks poking out the top.

Johnny Shim's skates.

Moni looked up, and as she caught his eye, she couldn't decide if she was the luckiest or unluckiest seventh grader in the whole entire world.

"Ta-da!" she said meekly, hoping he would somehow be impressed.

And then he smiled, his freckles only barely visible in the dim light.

"That was the wipeout of a lifetime, Moni Hayes."

Moni's stomach butterflied all the way from her belly button to her chest.

Johnny Shim reached out his arm, and Moni took his hand. It was chilly and dry. And wonderful. Johnny didn't help her up right away. In fact, her hand still in his, he crouched closer. He was wearing the flannel shirt he'd bought at Tina's the day before. It complemented his freckles and cloud hair nicely, Moni thought. She watched him open his mouth and take a breath in as if he were about to confess a secret, or at the very least say something incredibly important.

"OMG, Moni! Are you okay?" Grace cried, rushing up from behind them. "I saw you totally eat it out there!"

Johnny dropped Moni's hand—or was it Moni who dropped his?

"Yeah, all good. I'm made of steel," Moni joked,

flexing her biceps. She pushed herself to her feet and added, "Johnny, this is my best friend, Grace."

"The lucky recipient of your serenade," he said with a smile. "Hi."

"Hey," Grace responded with a little wave.

"Mega costumes," he added with a grin just big enough to show his dimple. Before Moni could thank him, the lights came up. "I'll see you around."

With that, Johnny slid away to meet his friends by the skate return area. The night was over.

"Should the fact that he saw me do that whole ridiculous serenade make me want to die?" Moni asked, turning to Grace.

"Um, Moni, that's a *good* thing. Don't you get it? He was watching you! Ignoring him completely worked!"

Moni sighed. She kind of got it. She leaned down to untie her skates. After her crash and the thrilling light-headed sensation that remained after Johnny's touch, she thought it wise to walk rather than skate back across the floor to retrieve her shoes.

"And you know what? Roxanna was definitely wrong about your Crush Necklace," Grace added.

"What do you mean?" Moni still felt a little

self-conscious about what her new necklace was evidently named. She didn't want to broadcast it.

"Look." Grace pointed to the charm that rested just above the zipper on her jacket.

The stone decorating the top of the key-shaped charm radiated an electric blue. "Cool . . . I guess. So do you think my singing voice has improved at all?" Moni asked as she unlaced one of her skates.

Grace laughed. "It's definitely better than your skating. You should really consider that helmet for next time."

"Can't argue with that," Moni said with a chuckle.

The same cliques that had whispered in closed circles two hours earlier now buzzed with excited chatter, intermingling and calling out last words before everyone went their separate ways. Moni felt a small swell of pride: It really was her serenade that broke the ice. For everyone. Moni and Grace slipped out of their heavy skates and walked in socks to the other side of the gym to retrieve their shoes.

She scanned for Johnny while she laced up her sneakers. His purple Converse weren't difficult to spot as he walked through the heavy blue doors, laughing with a few other boys. Right before he stepped out of sight, he suddenly stopped, turned, and caught her eye.

Moni gasped but managed to not look away.

"You're awesome, Moni Hayes," he called. Then he gave her two thumbs up before exiting.

Moni managed to give him a thumbs-up in return, but only after he'd gone.

"Way to play it cool, girl," Harley said, appearing from nowhere behind them. She nodded toward the door, where Johnny had been just seconds before. "Looks like you made a good impression!"

Moni swiveled her head and watched Harley pull Grace to her feet. Moni stayed on the floor, tying her other shoe. Raya joined but made no motion to hoist Moni up. That was fine; Moni could stand on her own.

"Didn't think you had it in you," Raya said matter-of-factly. "I'm kind of impressed. You really held it together until the end. I didn't see your fall, but I heard it. Sounded humiliating."

Moni didn't answer. It wasn't *that* bad, as it turned out.

"Okay, so we'll see y'all tomorrow for lake day?" Harley asked.

"Affirmative," Grace said with a grin.

Moni nodded, but her head was far from the upcoming lake day. She clasped her new good luck charm in her hand, the same hand that had just recently touched Johnny Shim's hand. One of the same hands that had given her the universally positive sign of a thumbs-up.

What a night. After Johnny Shim ignored her practically the whole time, she never would have expected the evening to end with such a bang. Or crash. Or Superman. Or whatever. Moni felt an additional swell of pride when she realized that perhaps she had indeed played it cool.

Seventh grade was intense.

Chapter Five

Moni's soaring good mood didn't last for long. She couldn't stop replaying the events of the evening over and over in her head. Specifically, the parts of the night where Johnny Shim was involved.

Back in Moni's living room, while Grace dished to Moni's mom about the details of their first skate night, Moni relived her personal highlights. She'd been very close to Johnny Shim's face. She'd noticed so many more details this time. The slight curve of Johnny's nose where she'd observed an extra-dense cluster of freckles. That piece of his hair that stuck out a little taller than the rest. The flutter deep in her chest when she realized he was reaching out his arm to help her—*her!*—to her feet. The slight twinkle in his eye (well, maybe it was the reflection of the disco ball, but whatever) when he gave her the oh-so-swoony double thumbs-up.

It was all so amazing she almost couldn't believe it had been real.

But when she and Grace retreated to her room to change into their pajamas and wash the glitter off their faces, doubts, like pesky little mosquitoes after a late summer rain, infiltrated Moni's thoughts.

Maybe the look in Johnny's eyes as he helped her up was pity. He'd said that was the wipeout of a lifetime. Did he think her fall was actually embarrassing, not cool? What if he didn't actually mean it when he'd shouted that she was awesome? Or in the hour and a half since, it was totally possible he'd changed his mind, right? Now that she really thought about it, his comment could easily have been sarcastic. He actually didn't *say* goodbye, after all.

Grace and Moni sat cross-legged on Moni's bed, eating mini marshmallows right out of the bag. Grace scrolled through her phone looking at all her photos from the night, while Moni toyed with the necklace around her neck, popping marshmallows into her mouth two at a time.

"What a roller coaster," Moni said as she exhaled.

"Huh?" Grace said without lifting her eyes from the screen.

"Nothing."

Moni reached for her bedside stand, where she'd placed the Crush Necklace box. Moni didn't usually sleep in jewelry. She should probably take the necklace off just in case the chain started to irritate her neck. But as she raised her hands to unhook the clasp, something inside the box caught her eye: a shimmer of gold.

She had to read the writing on the inside of the box twice before the words sank in.

Fun fact: This necklace is the key to your crush's heart.

"What are you mumbling about?" Grace asked.

Moni showed Grace the writing.

"Riddles are annoying," Moni said, mostly to mask the funny feeling in her chest. The "fun fact" was the part that really caused Moni's stomach to flip. It had to be a coincidence . . . right?

Moni watched her friend gently tug the satin away from the box at the corner. A tiny piece of paper poked out. Grace would make an excellent detective.

"No way," Moni said. "This box is a literal treasure hunt."

"Very on brand for Tina's Treasures, if you think about it," Grace added as she unfolded the paper for both of them to see.

The strip of paper—more like a tiny scroll—explained it all.

Fun fact fine print: This Crush Necklace is just for you (yes, you). The charm will activate when your crush is feeling you. You must be within touching distance of your crush for the Crush Necklace to work. The necklace is strong, but not that strong. Key: Dark blue = boo-hoo, bright blue = <.3

Moni looked down at the charm hanging around her neck. Boo-hoo, dark blue.

"There's a lot of attitude in that fine print," Moni murmured.

"It kind of sounds like you wrote it," Grace said, raising an eyebrow.

"What? You know that's not my handwriting." Moni insisted. "I couldn't make mine as old-fashionedy if I tried."

"Good point," Grace said, her signature *I'm thinking this through* look on her face. "If you're telling the truth—"

"I always tell the truth!" Moni exclaimed.

"I know," Grace said, still deep in thought. "So it's like the opposite of a mood ring. Necklace. Whatever Roxanna was talking about."

"It changes colors not based on my mood, but on my crush's—aka Johnny Shim's—feelings."

"That's . . ."

"Wild," Moni said, finishing Grace's thought for her. They stared at the scroll in wonder. Moni kept the key-shaped charm in her hand.

"Wild. But kind of great," Grace said carefully. Moni thought about it. *Would* that be great? "The mood necklace or whatever doesn't change based on *your* mood. It changes based on how the people you're with feel about you!" Grace was getting excited now. She stuffed no less than five mini marshmallows in her mouth. Hopefully she'd remember to chew. "Well, not other people, actually. Your crush."

Moni didn't respond right away. Grace's explanation hung in the air.

"Well?"

Moni thought Grace might actually explode with anticipation, so she started carefully. "Is that a good thing?"

"OMG, Ramona Dylan Hayes, this isn't a good thing," Grace said dramatically. "This is a *life-changing* thing!"

"But in a good way?"

"I'll spell it out for you. Who do you have a crush on?"

"Ugh, Johnny Shim, don't remind me!" Moni moaned, hiding her face in her hands.

"Exactly. And what is the most frustrating thing about having a crush on Johnny Shim?"

"One thing?"

"C'mon!"

"That sometimes he's into me and sometimes he isn't and I'm on an emotional roller coaster because I've never met anyone like him and he's such an amazing weirdo who I can't stop thinking about basically every second of every day and nothing makes sense!"

It felt good to get it all off her chest.

"Wow, okay, I think that was more than one thing, but you got it," Grace said, smiling. "The first part: You can't tell if he likes you or not. He's giving you mixed signals."

"It's so confusing! He ignored me all night, but then at the very end—"

"But now you have a way to clear up those mixed signals."

"To know if he likes me back," Moni said, finally catching on.

"Exactly!"

Grace flicked the charm hanging around Moni's neck with her finger. "This necklace can show you when he's into you."

Moni nodded, taking it all in.

"Doesn't that seem kind of like . . . I don't know, cheating?"

"No," Grace said quickly. "It's not cheating. Think of it as a tool."

"How will it help me, though?"

Grace thought for a second before she answered. "It turns bright blue when he likes you. So you just have to figure out what you do that can make it turn bright blue, and then keep doing those things."

"Simple as that?"

"Seems like it," Grace said, not picking up on Moni's skepticism.

"Do you think it's real?"

"Well, it was bright blue when we saw him at Tina's. And it was full-on radioactive after you crashed into him, which I totally would not have anticipated, but maybe you're charming when you fly through the air."

"Thank you, I think?"

"So . . . I think it's very possibly real!"

Moni hadn't seen Grace this excited in a while. She tried to match her best friend's energy.

"Okay!" Moni had always been gullible. Or optimistic, as she preferred to characterize it. She was tempted to stop herself from getting too excited, but the necklace really could help solve the mystery of Johnny Shim, and Grace was so pumped . . .

Grace's phone buzzed, and just like that she was distracted. She jotted down a text, pressed Send, and locked the screen in under three seconds flat.

"This could be cool. Like, really cool. Like crazy, fun cool. A necklace that will help you win the affections of your crush," Grace stated, as if she were talking to a toddler.

"Okay, so, if it's a beautiful, bright Caribbean blue, he loves me."

"Well, let's not get ahead of ourselves. If it's bright blue, he likes you." Sometimes Grace could be so pragmatic.

"All I have to do is make sure it stays bright blue, and I'm in business."

"You're in business."

"Crush Necklace business."

"Exactly."

After a few more handfuls of mini marshmallows, the girls said good night without brushing their teeth, Moni in her bed, Grace on a pile of couch pillows on the floor. As Moni slipped into dreams she wouldn't remember in the morning, the fun fact she'd forgotten to write in her journal tumbled around in her brain.

Maybe this necklace really was made for me, she thought as she drifted to sleep. *What a fun, fun fact.*

Chapter Six

Saturday mornings were for pancakes.

Sometimes Grace and Moni went to the diner where Moni's mom worked and got free ones, and sometimes they stayed at Moni's to cook them up themselves. They flipped a coin to decide. And then flipped another coin to determine who would run to the corner deli to pick up a carton of milk for the recipe. Moni lost both coin tosses.

So there she was at the local mini-mart, standing in aisle one. A catchy song by Boys Jump, another old band her mom just loved, played in the background. "Palomino" was the kind of song that was impossible not to get stuck in your head.

Moni absentmindedly sang along to the chorus as she picked up a jug of whole milk and headed to the counter to pay. Change jingled in the pocket of her cutoff shorts. She murmured the lyrics she heard playing over the tinny speakers. When the song was really good slash familiar, and when Moni happened to be in a place she pretty much knew like the back of her hand, like the Mason Mill mini-mart, she had a habit of closing her eyes while she sang along to the chorus. So far it had never been a particularly hazardous practice. So far.

"Palomino-o-o-o-o."

But the thing about singing with your eyes closed: You sometimes ran smack into people at the end of aisle one right by the tower of sparkling water. Long story short, Moni collided with that someone. And on that Saturday morning, just fourteen hours after the first Friday Night Skate of the year, Moni Hayes ran smack into Johnny Shim.

After the non-injury-inducing contact, she stood face-to-face, once again within touching and freckle-counting distance of her crush.

"Don't go-o-o." Even in crisis, Moni still hated to let a song lyric go unfinished. And the fact that Moni Hayes had run smack into Johnny Shim just fourteen hours after she had touched his fingertips with hers definitely qualified as a crisis. Or a miracle. Maybe both.

Moni's head spun. She was tempted to count his freckles. No. Not this time. She could say something funny instead! Something funny before he ran away and potentially never spoke to her again.

"Are you following me, Johnny Shim?" Shoot. Had she sounded too serious? Obviously she didn't think he was really following her. And maybe it would be cool if he came to the deli in hopes of seeing her. She wouldn't be mad about that one bit. Maybe he just lived nearby. That was probably it. "I mean, um . . . What are you doing here?"

Johnny's dimple flashed. What a dimple. "Scrambled-egg Saturday," he said, pointing to the egg carton in his hand.

"Pancake Saturday," Moni answered, wiggling her carton of milk.

He was wearing that shirt again.

"*You are here,*" Moni couldn't help but read aloud.

"*We* are here," Johnny corrected her. "Accuracy is underrated."

Moni couldn't have agreed more.

"We are here," Moni repeated, without knowing what to say next. How come she seemed to lose her grasp on the English language when she was within touching and freckle-counting distance of Johnny Shim?

"Your serenade yesterday was really mega. Best part of the skate night for sure."

"I mean, sometimes the right song comes on and you just can't stop yourself, you know? Hopefully I'll get better at skating soon because I have all sorts of floor burn on my elbows." Moni paused to catch her breath.

Boys Jump continued to play in the background.

"Don't take my heart . . ." Moni sang. At that moment, she desperately wished literally any other song were playing. Now Johnny Shim must think he was stealing her heart.

"Palomino-o-o," Johnny Shim sang softly. "My mom loves this song."

"Mine, too!" The words practically exploded out of Moni's mouth. She couldn't believe how much they had in common! "Very catchy," Moni added.

For a beat, Moni watched Johnny watch her. What was he thinking?

Finally he said, "I think you might be magic, Moni Hayes."

Moni was speechless. Magic?! Now, *that* was a

compliment. Swoon central. "Like, seriously. I think your necklace is alive." Moni looked down, but before she was able to pull the charm away from her neck enough to see, Johnny clarified, "It literally turned bright blue right before my eyes. How did it do that?"

Moni's gut reaction was to panic. Bright blue was a good thing. Right? But he wasn't supposed to notice that the necklace changed colors. That the necklace was magic. A magic Crush Necklace. Right? Right! This could be bad—real bad. She had to change the subject.

"It's definitely not magic! No magic around here, no way!" Moni blurted.

"Are you sure?" Johnny asked, smiling. Moni couldn't be certain if he was joking or not, but she couldn't risk it.

"Lake day!" Moni exclaimed, changing the subject. Ugh. She had to get better at speaking in complete sentences mid-panic.

"Lake day?" Johnny asked.

"Lake day!"

Moni's heartbeat had yet to decelerate. She had to calm down. There was a chance she'd been shouting at him, though she couldn't be certain

"Lake day," she repeated, this time closer to a whisper. "Today. We're going. Wanna come?"

Moni clutched the charm in her hand and gave it a small pulse while she waited for Johnny Shim to respond. And, of course, counted his freckles.

One . . . two . . . three . . .

Moni was almost in double digits by the time Johnny Shim finally opened his mouth to speak.

Chapter Seven

"I'm doomed," Moni shouted toward the partly cloudy sky above.

After Moni had identified a total of eleven freckles on Johnny Shim's face (some old, some new), he finally said yes to the lake hang (to be accurate, he'd said "surely"—even the way he accepted invitations was thrilling—swoon-o-rama!). Moni had felt elated, but only for a moment. Then reality set in.

"What do I do when he actually gets here? What do I say? What if he changes his mind? What if he gets a sunburn and then blames me for it and hates me forever?"

Moni paced back and forth in front of four neatly placed beach towels, chewing the last of a poppy seed bagel she'd brought as a post-pancake snack. The sand felt like hot loaves of bread on Moni's bare feet. Moni had finally spilled the beans to Grace,

Harley, and Raya once they'd arrived at the lake. She'd managed to last an entire short stack of pancakes plus the twenty-minute walk to the lake without letting it slip. Moni wasn't trying to keep it a secret, especially not from Grace, but saying "Johnny Shim will be hanging at the lake with us today" made it all real. And scary. But as the quad neared the lakeshore, the sun rose higher (and hotter) in the sky, and Moni's adrenaline from the mini-mart amplified to jitterbug-level nerves. In one long, single breath, she explained how she had run into Johnny Shim while buying milk and how she'd invited him to come to the lake day without thinking through the repercussions. Or the possibility that he really might come. Now the reality that her crush was coming to hang at the lake in T-minus a few minutes had set in. Moni needed all the moral support she could get.

"Calm down, you are so not doomed," Grace assured her.

"Potentially the opposite of doomed," Harley said as she pulled magazines from her bag.

"He would get a sunburn," Raya muttered.

Moni ignored Raya's dig. "Okay, fine. Not in a cosmic sense, but in a *My crush is coming to the lake to hang out and I don't know how to handle it* sense, yes. One hundred percent, zombie apocalypse, aliens invading the Earth, DOOMED."

Grace looked at Moni skeptically.

"How do I fix this?" Moni demanded.

"Nothing is broken, except for potentially your mind," Grace confirmed. "Pretty bold move, Moni."

Her awkward lake-day invitation had been bold, now that Grace mentioned it, even if it manifested because of the need to get Johnny's attention off her necklace.

The necklace! That was also a source of Moni's preoccupation. *Your necklace is alive.* Johnny Shim's observation ran on Repeat in her head. The implications both excited and terrified her.

"Moni, you're a monster, making the first move." Raya said, sounding almost impressed. "I didn't think you had it in you,"

"Very commendable," Harley agreed, attention more focused on putting on sunscreen than the conversation, it seemed.

"I think it was a mistake. Like, for sure a mistake. Major, major, major mistake," Moni said, continuing to pace.

"Hey, watch your stomping, you're getting sand, or dirt, or whatever this stuff is all up on me," Raya complained.

Dirt-sand. The sediment on the shore of Bell Lake wasn't necessarily dirt but wasn't quite sand, either. A major plus of living in Mason Mill was the beach access. Lake-beach access, to be precise. It was like a big public swimming pool, but with more frogs, motorboats owned by people from Atlanta, and less fluorescent water. *Au naturel*, as Raya might say.

Though Labor Day had already come and gone, the air still felt convincingly like summer. In Mason Mill, temperatures sometimes reached the eighties through Halloween. But as it was still the first weeks of school in September, the weekend was scorching.

"Just close your eyes and take a breath, girlfriend," Raya instructed.

Summer lake vibes usually put Moni at ease, and as she followed Raya's command and fluttered her eyes shut, the sounds of kids splashing and parents gossiping and the delicious smell of grease from the snack bar momentarily transported Moni back to a different time when Crush Necklaces, soccer girls, and Johnny Shims didn't exist.

Ah, to go back to sixth grade, when life was simple.

"I can't with this sunscreen. I'm jumping in," Harley declared. Moni opened her eyes to see Raya racing toward the water after her. Soccer girls sure had speed.

"Shall we?" Grace dared, already taking a step toward the water.

"Wait," Moni said, grabbing her best friend's arm. "You know the real reason I asked Johnny to the lake?"

"Go on," Grace said, intrigued.

"My necklace," Moni whispered, taking hold of the charm. "Johnny called it out for turning bright blue. Before his eyes."

"Whoa."

"It really works. The necklace knows," Moni said, voice still barely audible. "But how?"

"This is amazing! Who cares how it knows," Grace whispered more loudly than she should have, starting to get excited. "It just knows!"

"The necklace knows!" Moni said.

"The necklace knows, the necklace knows!" the girls whisper-chanted in unison. They'd always loved a good chant, whether it was whispered or screamed at the top of their lungs. Moni didn't know if she was most excited about the presence of proven crush-related magic dangling right there around her neck or if sharing a moment with her favorite friend in the world was the best medicine for, well, just about anything.

"Promise you won't tell Harley and Raya about my necklace?" Moni asked, suddenly serious. Having something that belonged to her and Grace alone felt absolutely essential.

"Promise."

Moni believed her. Neither Moni nor Grace had ever broken a promise. Together, they ran into the lake, splashing until they dove headfirst into the murky, tepid water.

After their dip, the girls air-dried on their towels.

Harley put on her sunglasses. "When he comes—"

"*If* he comes," Moni interrupted.

"*When* he comes," Grace insisted. "He's not the flaking type, I can tell."

"Agreed," Harley said, nodding. "So, when he comes, don't act too eager."

"Right," Raya confirmed. "Like, don't get over-excited about the whole thing."

"But I am excited," Moni admitted. *And terrified,*

Moni thought. Yes, excitement and terror sure seemed to go hand in hand when crushes (and Crush Necklaces) were involved.

"That's so not the point," Raya said. "You can *be* excited, duh. But don't *show* him how excited you are."

"Okay," Moni said, trying to wrap her head around all this new information. "Don't act too eager."

"Exactly."

"It really works like a charm," Harley confirmed.

Moni clasped her hand over her necklace and met Grace's eyes. Grace nodded and gave her a little smile. Moni smiled back. She felt better. She could do this. She just needed to contain any and all excitement in Johnny Shim's presence. That was doable, right? And if her charm turned bright blue, then she would know that Harley and Raya's advice was good *and* Johnny was into her. Confirmation. Two birds, one stone.

This was going to be fine. Maybe even fun.

Let the games begin!

Twenty minutes later, Johnny had yet to arrive and Moni was not exactly having fun. Moni feared he might actually be the flaking type after all. In an effort to be a good sport, Moni joined Harley, Raya, and Grace by the water's edge, passing the soccer ball around in a small circle while gossiping more about the events of skate night.

"Much Love is such a flirt," Raya gushed. Moni thought she detected a blush. Maybe it was just the sun.

"Surprise, surprise, his name is Much Love," Moni said glumly.

"A nickname for Mycah," Raya added sharply, as if Moni had insulted him. Which maybe she had.

Raya passed the ball hard across the circle to Harley, who launched it back equally as hard to Grace, bouncing it off her shins and unexpectedly toward Moni. The ball rolled over the lumpy dirt-sand, suddenly taking an odd bounce right as Moni's foot made contact.

"Ow!" she cried as the sphere jammed into her big toe. Stupid soccer.

"Moni, you can't kick with your toe," Grace chided.

Moni picked up the ball and rolled it across the circle to Raya. "I'm just gonna ice this off," Moni said, hobbling toward the water's edge. The lake that had been heating under the hot Georgia sun for four months, but whatever. Nobody immediately called her out.

"Hey, are you okay?" Grace asked, wading out to Moni's side a moment later. The water hit Moni's belly button, but only the tops of Grace's thighs. Maybe seventh grade would be more manageable if Moni were several inches taller.

No. That was dumb. Several inches wouldn't change anything.

"I'm fine. I just . . . I guess all this crush stuff and what I'm supposed to do about it is stressing me out. It's so complicated."

"Just be yourself. You're the best!"

"Right." Moni dug her throbbing big toe into the muddy lakebed.

"Well, well, well." Grace gently elbowed Moni in the ribs and then gestured toward the shore. "I think your day is about to get that much better."

Purple Converse on the dirt-sand, giant sun hat, and cool as a glass of hibiscus iced tea: It was Johnny Shim.

Moni's stomach triple-flipped as she jumped up and waved. She was about to call out when Grace interjected.

"Not too much enthusiasm!" she whispered, even though nobody was in earshot. Darn. Okay. Moni dropped her hand and put on her best bored face. "I doubt he can see your totally over-the-top expression from the shore."

Moni exaggerated even more, dropping her head to one side and sticking her tongue out. Grace gave Moni a playful splash, and Moni giggled. Part of her wanted to horse around in the lake with Grace all day and forget that the oh-so-cute and oh-so-tardy Johnny Shim was only twenty feet away.

Most of her. But not all of her. She watched Johnny sit down and not unlace his purple Converse.

"You got this. Remember, the necklace," Grace insisted.

Moni looked down at the charm. With the scorch from the sun and the heat of the water, the necklace around her neck felt heavier than usual. The stone was dark blue, just like her eyes, just like the lake water, just like—

"Heads up!" Harley shouted.

Moni saw the torpedoing soccer ball just in time to duck out of the way. Raya's body followed right behind. Moni dodged to the left to avoid being tackled. Moni was soaked, but Raya had caught the ball in her outstretched arms.

"Backup goalie material right here!" she exclaimed when she resurfaced.

"Nice!" Harley cheered as she rushed into the water to meet them.

"Go, I'll stall them out here to give y'all some privacy," Grace said softly, pushing Moni toward the shore. "Good luck!"

Moni gave Grace a modest smile and walked out of the water. Johnny waved as she walked his way. Moni smiled but didn't wave back.

"Hi," Moni said, toweling off. Johnny Shim had taken a seat on the dirt-sand. No towel. His hat was even bigger close up. "You made it."

"I made it," he said with a smile.

Moni sat down next to him. She wiggled her toes until they disappeared underneath the dirt-sand. Moni didn't know what to say next. So she said the first thing that came to mind.

"I really like your hat," she said, because she did.

Though she sat several feet away from him, the tan brim nearly brushed her shoulder.

"Thanks. It's effective."

Moni turned to look him in the eye. His freckles looked darker in the sunlight. Effective!

"For your freckles!" Moni exclaimed.

"I've got a lot."

"More than I can count!"

Moni clamped her hand over her mouth. She'd said too much. Way, way too much.

"That sounds accurate," Johnny Shim said with a smile. "But I've never tried counting them."

"Neither have I," Moni said quickly.

"Maybe I should," he added.

Moni nodded as non-eagerly as she could manage.

They sat in silence for a bit. Moni wiggled her toes underneath the dirt-sand and tried not to look enthusiastic, eager, or anything that could be mistaken for excitement. That was easier to do, she found, if a part of her was wiggling.

Finally, after what felt like twenty-four hours, Johnny Shim said, "Tell me something good, Moni Hayes."

Something good. What, according to Johnny Shim, was good? Again, Moni blurted the first thing that came to mind.

"Bananas contain a natural chemical that makes people feel happy."

"That's convenient."

"Very," Moni agreed. "Especially if you like banana pancakes."

"Who doesn't?"

"Exactly!" Shoot. Moni had gotten too excited again. "I mean, they're all right. Nothing too special."

Johnny pulled a tube of sunscreen from his pocket and began applying it to his face. A smear of the white lotion, Moni noticed, stuck to a few of his longest eyelashes.

"Any good rocks to paint today?" she asked.

"That is a truly excellent question. You listen with your eyes and your ears, don't you, Moni Hayes?"

"Maybe. Yes. I never thought about it before."

"I think you do. I learned about listening with your eyes from my dad. He used to be an actor before he decided his heart belonged to commercial real estate."

"Oh" was all Moni could manage.

"Yeah. But he learned how to listen with his ears and his eyes when he performed Shakespeare back when he was young. It's an interesting concept. I try to practice it whenever I can."

"Good idea."

"I think you might do it naturally," Johnny added. "You're very good at eye contact. That's not a common quality."

Moni blushed. Then she remembered her necklace and glanced down, moving her head as little as possible in the process. Out of the bottom of her eye she saw that, without a doubt, the charm glowed a blue as bright as an artificially flavored Popsicle.

Moni's heart cartwheeled. She managed not to smile too big. She hoped.

What next? Moni thought to ask about his recent dreams. Would that definitely count as enthusiastic? She didn't want to risk the charm returning back to that cold, boo-hoo dark blue. As if on cue, Moni noticed Grace and company returning from their swim. Moni was smart enough to know that a conversation about dreams with Johnny Shim was best suited for their ears alone.

Moni introduced Johnny Shim to the others when they arrived. Because she had good manners.

Lake day resumed. Harley treated everyone to grilled cheese and an order of chicken fingers to share. Moni's and Johnny's hands touched when they dipped their halves of chicken finger into barbecue sauce at the same time. Moni didn't dare catch his eye. She continued to check in with her necklace when she remembered. Which, admittedly, wasn't a lot. Every time she did look, it was the color of her eyes. Boo. Maybe she'd missed a flash of bright blue. She'd have to ask Grace later. Grace, she trusted, had her eyes trained on Moni's necklace the entire afternoon.

A few hours later, as thunderstorm clouds approached with convincing certainty, everyone gathered their gear to go home. Johnny Shim didn't have to do much packing—he'd kept on his shoes and hat the entire time.

"I don't really do water," he'd said when Raya asked him why he didn't swim.

Moni saw Raya roll her eyes. She hoped Johnny hadn't seen because, as she was learning, a Raya eye roll was sharper than a fang.

When the first drops plopped from the sky, every-one scattered. Grace had to go home to feed both her cat and her baby sister, but promised to call later. Moni watched Harley and Raya scamper off down a tree-lined path they insisted was a shortcut of some sort. Moni and Johnny walked to the edge of the lake parking lot together. When the gravel smoothed to asphalt, Moni turned right to head to her apartment, and Johnny Shim started to turn left.

"Sorry you don't do water," Moni said as she gave Johnny an extremely cumbersome side hug before they split ways.

"Sorry I didn't bring any bananas."

Moni laughed out loud.

Just moments later, after they'd said goodbye and Moni was alone, she noticed her charm still shined an eager, bright blue.

Despite the light rain, Moni walked home at a lei-surely pace, thinking about the afternoon: the ups, the downs, the highs and lows. For the first time all day, she felt like she had space to breathe. When Moni reached to make sure the charm on her necklace remained, she found that the top of the key rested perfectly in the little dip between her collarbones.

Grace was right. This Crush Necklace thing was amazing. *More than amazing*, Moni thought. The Crush Necklace was incredible. A lifesaver. Everything she needed and more. The Crush Necklace was, in fact, the rule book that Moni had craved ever since the day Grace returned from soccer camp and seventh grade had begun. Finally, Moni had a compass to guide her.

Chapter Eight

The video call came that evening, just as Moni was finishing her Popsicle. Her second Popsicle, to be exact. She lay across her bed on her stomach, propped up by her elbows. She was skilled at eating Popsicles in bed without letting any of the runoff drip onto her blanket. She licked the last of the sticky electric blue sugar syrup from the stick and dropped it onto her bedside table next to the first and pressed Accept on the video call from Grace. Had she known who all would be on the other end, she may have . . . well, she would have remembered that the red, white, and blue of a firecracker Popsicle turned her tongue a flushed purple. After two firecrackers, her mouth appeared a deep violet. When she saw Harley and Raya were also on the video call, Moni furiously rubbed her lips against the back of her hand. It sort of worked.

"Gotta recap," Harley said once they were all connected.

Moni quickly gathered that after any remotely social event, Harley and Raya (and now Grace) liked to talk about and then analyze every moment that went down.

"Very solid lake hang," Harley assessed.

"The most solid," Raya echoed.

"So much fun," Grace said.

"Mega." Moni liked the way that word sounded. It felt like just the right descriptor.

"So, I'm not going to lie, that Johnny Shim dude is a total weirdo," Raya started.

Harley interrupted before Raya could continue. "Cute, though. For sure cute."

"Sure. How you managed to see his face under that hat . . . literally the size of a seventy-pound mammal," Raya said.

Raya was intense, and maybe a little mean, but also not *not* funny. Girl had wit, which Moni couldn't help but admire.

"I hear medium-sized-mammal hats are all the rage in Paris," Moni joked.

"Whatever. My point is, I do think he's into you.

And because I am an angel, I did you a favor." Just then a text from Raya popped up on Moni's screen. A phone number.

"How did you—"

Raya cut her off. "When there's a will, there's a way. And when you know Tati, there's a faster way. You're welcome. Use it wisely."

Moni gazed down at the phone number. Johnny Shim's phone number. Right there before her. It felt both precious and dangerous.

"I told you that whole not-being-too-excited thing works," Raya said proudly.

"Like a charm," Harley said in a singsong voice. "Speaking of charms, I thought that one on your necklace was neon blue, not dark blue."

Moni looked down to check for herself. Dark blue. Obviously. Johnny wasn't there in her living room with her.

"Possibly," Moni said, trying to play it off.

Moni racked her brain for excuses about the changing color, so she didn't hear her mom coming through the open bedroom door behind her. In fact, she only noticed she was there when she saw her reflection in the small mirrored square on the video call.

"Ramona Dylan Love Straw Hayes—"

"Mom, don't call me—" *Love Straw* was what Moni was going to say. But Nikki Hayes was as quick with her words as her daughter.

"I know you aren't leaving those sticky poison Popsicle sticks on your table like that."

Moni's mom wasn't much for scolding, but that summer they'd had ants. Probably because Moni loved Popsicles and left the sticks all over the place. In her mind, since the sticks were wood and biodegradable, it wasn't a big deal. Plus, she licked the Popsicle syrup clean off those suckers, so she wasn't necessarily convinced the ants were her doing. Her mom strongly disagreed.

"Sorry, sorry, I'll throw them out in a sec!" Moni promised.

"Look at this! Three-way calling really is so much more advanced now!" Moni's mom ducked her way into the frame at a crooked angle and waved at the girls. Even though Moni's mom was very young and very hip, certain totally normal things, like basic technology, seemed beyond her basic comprehension.

"Hey, Nikki," Harley said quickly. If Moni didn't

know better, she'd say Harley was almost nervous around her mom. But not in the way that most kids were nervous around adults. Like she wanted to impress her. It annoyed Moni.

"Hey, girls!"

Moni shifted the screen so her mom cut out of the frame, shooing her with a flutter of her feet.

"Some privacy, please!" she whispered.

"Well, excuse me, Miss Thang," Moni's mom said, putting her hands up. "I guess I'm going to have to eat all this monster pie I liberated from work by myself."

Shoot. Moni just loved monster pie.

"Okay, I'll be out in a minute!" she said. Then mouthed, *Sorry*, making sure the phone screen momentarily pointed toward her pillow.

"Bye, ladies," Moni's mom shouted in the general direction of Moni's phone, and then to Moni, "If you don't get your tail out here soon, I'm taking all the pecans off the top for myself."

Women in the Hayes family were powerless against pecans. Pecans on top of monster pie? Very much a double kryptonite.

"Your mom is, like, so cool," Harley said when Moni's mom had left and the screen once again focused on Moni's purple-lipped face.

"Yep, the coolest," Moni said, trying to hide her irritation.

"Y'all, Much Love just sent me a message with the kapow emoji," Raya announced.

"Ooh, I love that emoji," Harley exclaimed.

"I know, it's kind of the best one, right? Well done, Much Love."

"The what emoji?" Moni asked.

"The one that looks like a tiny cartoon explosion," Grace informed. "Duh."

"Right. Duh," Moni said.

All in all, the recap was relatively quick. Everyone was sad that the future lake beach outings were coming to an end now that summer was over. Though practices with Belleayre Fire had paused since the end of team camp, the school soccer season had just begun. Harley, Raya, and Grace anticipated a fitness test at soccer practice that week, which was going to be a nightmare. Moni didn't add much to the conversation. She'd only ever video-chatted with Grace once. Video chats were weird. Moni wasn't sure if she was supposed to look at the person speaking the entire time. Nobody else really did, but when she didn't, she found it too hard to remember to pay attention.

The moment they all hung up, Moni called Grace back. A regular voice call this time. She picked up on the first ring.

"So, that was intense," Moni said, without saying hi.

Grace chuckled. "Yeah. They got that video thing down pat."

"Right, necklace recap, then." Moni shut her bedroom door, just in case her mom was listening or something. Did her mom do that? Even if Nikki Hayes was the coolest, official Crush Necklace talk called for privacy.

"So your necklace was kind of blowing up!" Grace confirmed.

"Right?! I noticed it was bright blue after I asked Johnny if there were any good rocks to paint."

"Wow, that did it for him. He is so . . ." Grace paused, as if searching for the perfect word. "Unique."

"You mean swoonable?"

"Sure. Yes," Grace said with a laugh. "Whatever floats your boat."

Moni flopped back onto her bed and smiled.

"I also noticed it was bright blue when you informed everyone that chicken fingers without ranch dressing are worthless."

"That is a scientific fact. I can't believe Harley even dared to argue with me."

"And it was also bright blue after those annoying-slash-cute teenage boys hit you on the head with a Frisbee."

"When I got Frisbee assaulted or after when I threw the evil Frisbee onto the roof of the snack bar, where hopefully it will remain until the end of time?"

"I think the two kind of blended together," Grace said. Moni could practically hear her eye roll through the phone.

"What about all the times I did the whole don't-act-too-excited thing?" Grace paused to think about it for a moment. "Wait, maybe I should write all this down. It's a lot to keep track of."

"Good idea," Grace agreed. Moni reached for her fun fact journal underneath her pillow. That would have to double as the official Crush Necklace journal.

"Well, most of that stuff happened while you weren't really paying attention to him. Which you did a pretty good job of, to be honest."

"Thanks. It was kind of easy because I felt awkward around him with everyone watching."

"Everyone was not watching."

"You know what I mean," Moni said.

"I do. So yeah, I'd say that the whole don't-get-excited-around-him thing was effective. As proven by your treasured Crush Necklace," Grace said.

"Anything else?" So far these instances of the necklace were affirming but not mind-blowing.

"Yes, actually. When I called you out for having that rogue poppy seed in your teeth."

"I knew you were being obvious about that!"

"You should really be thanking me. When you asked if it made you look like a pirate, the necklace popped off."

"Wow, I never would have guessed that one." Moni was quite relieved, actually. She'd been cursing that lodged poppy seed ever since Grace pointed it out. Nothing worse than food stuck in your teeth and not knowing. Especially poppy seeds. At least now she knew that it hadn't ruined everything between her and the fantastic Johnny Shim. Thanks, Crush Necklace!

"Yes, I thought that was interesting, too."

Moni adopted what she considered to be her best scientist voice. "So the conclusions we can draw from phase one of this experiment are as follows." She paused, waiting for Grace to fill in the blank. Grace didn't make a peep. Up to Moni. "It seems like Johnny Shim likes when I talk to him about his art, ruin disc games, and look like a fool."

"Looks like it."

"I'd say inconclusive so far."

"We'll keep experimenting. You'll have more chances at school."

"Good point."

"Moni, baby, I'm getting hungry!" a muffled voice called from the other side of the door.

"Okay, go eat pie," Grace groaned. "Ugh, you're so lucky. We're having some sort of meat stew tonight. Later!"

"Later, love you!"

"Love you."

Moni tossed her phone down on her bed and bopped into the kitchen. Her mom sat at the table, open textbook in front of her, untouched monster pie in the center. Two forks lay crisscrossed next to the dessert.

"I'm thinking we go plateless," Moni's mom said as Moni approached. "Dare we?"

"Duh."

They dug in. It wasn't until the post-sugar-rush stomachache kicked in that Moni considered the possibility that while the Crush Necklace had answered three very important questions that day, it also seemed to generate three hundred more. Did Johnny Shim like to see her get hit in the head with sports objects or throw sports objects far away? No way to know. Did he like ranch dressing, or did he like to see her argue about ranch dressing? Unclear. Did Johnny Shim like poppy seeds or just girls who reminded him of pirates? Possibly both.

All and all, four total bright blue moments seemed pretty good. Not that Moni had anything to compare it to. Maybe four wasn't good. Should the Crush Necklace have been bright blue the entire time? She wished the instructions had been a little more specific.

Moni would just have to pay more attention, she resolved. Be like Grace—always remember the necklace. She could do that, right?

The grumble of chocolate chips, corn syrup, graham cracker crust, and pecans in her stomach told her that yes, yes she could.

Chapter Nine

Sundays were for homework. That's how Moni liked it. She saved science until last because it was her favorite. Science Sundays. Science comforted Moni ever since she could remember. She liked that if you followed all the instructions, the outcome was inevitable, predictable. Moni's mom had worked her magic to (finally) get Sundays off, so they spent the afternoons listening to a carefully curated '90s playlist: Backstreet Boys, Heat Squad, Spice Girls, 98 Degrees, Boys Jump, and the Verge, among others. Moni's mom had started taking online business classes a year ago, chipping away one credit at a time, she liked to say. If all went as planned, she would have a business degree by the time Moni started high school. And then, together, they would rule the world.

"You sure are getting a lot of texts, Love Straw," her mom said, stretching her arms overhead. Moni's mom always did her work on the side of the couch closest to the window, and Moni did hers on the floor in front of the TV.

"Grace added me to this group text with Harley and Raya," Moni said. Though she felt great when the add happened—like access to a private garden—now it was almost annoying. Almost. It's like those girls were all physically attached to their phones. They seemed to text nonstop. One minute it was What flavor ice cream to get???, the next, Rain clouds are such a bummmmmer. That afternoon Harley had asked, How do I find the YouTube video about the living juicebox again? As much as it wasn't Moni's vibe to communicate with such frequency, now that she was in the text group, she didn't want them to regret including her. She dutifully responded when necessary, and even offered Ugh, homework (which garnered an immediate flurry of commiserating responses).

"It's cool you're meeting new people this year," Moni's mom murmured. "How about a fun fact before I hit the hay?"

"Hmmm." Moni referenced her fun fact journal, which she'd kept concealed beneath her science folder. Amid the fun facts was the list she'd started of the instances her necklace had turned bright blue. Seeing that list again stressed her out. She flipped to the next page. "Boys take up a lot of space," Moni blurted.

Moni's mom chuckled.

"If you let them, Love Straw. Only if you let them."

Moni thought about that and wrote down her fun fact and her mom's response on the top of a fresh, blank page.

Before she got into bed, as Moni plugged in her phone to charge for the night, Moni noticed the Popsicle sticks that were now probably permanently attached to her bedside table. Which gave her an idea. A possibly brilliant idea.

I bet Popsicle sticks are good for dreams too zzzzzzzzzz —Moni Hayes.

Her finger hovered over the Send button after she'd typed the message out. Should she add a period? An exclamation point? The cartwheel emoji? Was adding her name to the end too formal—was that really the best way to identify herself? She could debate these questions for hours, she realized.

Moni pressed Send and then got into bed.

Before the spot on the mattress beneath her had a chance to warm, she got up and walked back to her phone. She typed in the lollipop emoji. Then reconsidered and deleted it. Maybe it would be better to play it safe. The kapow emoji. Moni typed one in. But not too safe. Moni added a second. And then a third, because three kapow emojis were funnier than just two.

Third one's a charm. A charm on a Crush Necklace.

Moni pressed Send, felt that shiver of electricity in her chest, turned her phone to silent, and got back into bed. She pulled the covers up all the way to her nose, and though she didn't notice, any witness could see the tips of her toes wiggling under her thin blanket. She fell asleep on her side, one hand peacefully placed under her head, the other enclosing the charm necklace around her neck.

Chapter ten

"You did *what*?" Raya asked after school the next day.

Moni loitered after school with Harley, Raya, and Grace by the Music Box Steps. The soccer girls had half an hour to kill before practice. Moni had nowhere to be. She could probably benefit from an after-school activity, she realized. She was beginning to feel like a soccer groupie.

The Music Box Steps: a fancy name for the fire escape on the right side of the main school entrance. Nobody seemed to know why the steps had been named such, but everybody knew that's what they were called. Seventh graders got the Music Box Steps and surrounding area, eighth graders claimed the luxurious Goose Benches, and sixth graders were left to fend for themselves. No geese or music boxes were harmed in the naming of said locations.

"I just texted him about something I thought he'd like," Moni said defensively. "I guess you could say it's like an inside joke. Well, not a joke. A conversation. A thing."

"What did he say?"

"Yup, yup."

"And this text came in when?" Harley asked.

"Lunch," Grace answered for her, inserting herself into the conversation.

"Wow," Harley marveled.

"How'd he spell it—the *yups*?" Raya asked. Moni showed her. "Interesting. Comma, no period, very low-key spelling. Finishing with an exclamation point would have been the considerate thing to do."

"I mean, really," Harley added.

"Sometimes I wish I didn't have a phone," Moni sighed. She meant it. "My gut told me we'd get a nice little chat going with the inside joke—I mean, *thing*—I texted about." What Moni didn't say was that all the flashes of bright blue from lake day had (perhaps falsely) bolstered her confidence.

"Oh, Moni, Moni, Moni. Have we taught you nothing?" Raya nearly screamed. Moni worried Raya might get her arms tangled up, she was waving them so frantically. "The first lesson being that you probably shouldn't follow your instincts. At least when boys are concerned. Science, or whatever subjects you're good at, yes. Boys, no, no, no."

"That's basically breaking the number one rule, which is don't seem too available. Remember, boys are dumber than honeybees," Harley explained in a less hysterical tone.

"Honeybees are very smart, actually. They live in eusocial colonies," Moni recited from memory. The seventh-grade eco science curriculum was proving to be quite fascinating.

"You are such a dork," Raya said, shaking her head. Moni also saw her mouth twist into a smile that could only be described as almost affectionate. So Moni chose to take her comment as a compliment.

"Thank you," she chirped.

"Moni, listen to them," Grace pleaded.

Moni bit her tongue.

"I'll go over this again," Raya said. "Courtesy of my sometimes-bratty but mostly awesome older sister: One, don't get too excited. Two, don't text him first, and if he doesn't respond in a timely manner or with appropriate punctuation, definitely don't text him again. Three, boys can't handle losing. They're babies and it sucks, but it's true. Four, let him see you having fun. That's very important. Are you writing this down?" Moni was actually jotting a note to include the bit about honeybees in her fun fact journal when she got home. Might as well jot down these suggestions, too, while she was at it. "Take notes. Harley, Grace, what am I missing?"

"I think you nailed it," Harley chimed.

"Totally nailed it," Grace confirmed.

"What about all the other stuff that pertains to humans in general, like being a good listener?" Moni asked, remembering the compliment Johnny had given her at the lake a few days earlier. "And having a sense of humor, and being considerate and stuff?"

Raya rolled her eyes. "Yeah, yeah, that's child's play. We're in seventh grade now. Big leagues."

Harley nodded.

"The big leagues," Grace said pointedly, lest Moni forget.

"Time to take matters into your own hands," Raya declared.

"Speaking of, I'll literally pay someone to write

this essay for me," Harley complained. "It's, like, physically and emotionally impossible for me to get the words on the page."

"Same, except for science and it's actually some lab report thing about an experiment or something." Raya sighed, deflated. "Do you think if I just close my eyes, it will go away?" Raya forced her eyes shut and tensed her face.

"Yes. Definitely," Moni confirmed.

Grace gave her a playful swat.

"C'mon, let's go," Harley said, hoisting her backpack over one shoulder and her soccer bag over the other. "If we're late to practice . . . sprints!"

"I can't believe we have our first game in a week. If I don't start, I'm going to be so depressed I'll be forced to do my science homework," Raya moaned.

"Well, that will be the day," Moni whispered to Grace. They shared a quick giggle before Grace caught up to Harley, who led the way to the soccer field.

Moni stood up to walk home when Raya called her name. Well, sort of her name.

"Monilee."

"Huh? Mon-i-what?"

"That's what I'm calling you now." Raya was a weirdo, too. "Johnny's text is ridiculous and completely inconsiderate. But I think he's all about it, still. I really do. Maybe he forgot to turn on his phone."

"He was being attacked by killer ants!" Moni suggested.

"Sure. Or that. There's no way to know what he was thinking. You don't need to wait around for him. If you're into it, make it happen, Monilee. You have four weeks until the next Friday Night Skate. You got this. Don't give up hope. If your hat-wearing goofball isn't into you, I think he's dumb, and we will still triumph like the awesome, magnificent seventh-grade gals we are. Got it?"

"Got it. Thanks. I think."

"Don't mention it."

Raya trotted off after Grace and Harley. Moni hung back on the benches. Despite Raya's fairly confusing assessment of Moni's love life, Moni was both surprised by and appreciated her loyalty.

Plus, Moni wasn't one to just hope her crush was still into her, especially when there was, in fact, a way she could know. She tugged at the key-shaped charm dangling from her neck, wiggled her toes, and smiled.

Chapter Eleven

Moni had a plan. Special Operation Sneak Attack, she called it. It was simple. In theory.

She wanted to see if her necklace would turn bright blue, but she needed to be near Johnny in order for the stone to activate. Easier said than done, as they only had one class together: gym. Still, Moni was not deterred.

Getting within touching distance of Johnny Shim proved to be a borderline athletic experience.

Moni knew that after second period, Johnny Shim walked by room 201 on his way to math. She knew this because after second period, Moni Hayes walked by 201 from the opposite direction, on her way to science. In order to catch him between bells and still make it back to science class on time (Ms. Starks was lecturing on Arctic ecosystems and she didn't want to miss a minute), Moni had to hustle.

As first period ended and dozens of students dumped into the narrow halls, Moni quickly spotted a poof of cloud hair a school bus's distance in front of her.

Go time.

"Watch it!" the guy who always wore red shorts said as she bumped his shoulder.

"Sorry," she mumbled. Did he really have to move that slowly? It was obvious she had somewhere to be!

Moni continued to bob and weave through the crowd, stepping on at least half a dozen feet.

"Hey! New sneakers, hello!" a particularly big-footed boy snapped.

"Sorry, sorry, sorry," Moni repeated as she pressed on.

Moni checked the clock on the wall. Two minutes until third period. She had to catch him. Moni Hayes would not be deterred; she was the kind of girl who always rose to a challenge. So she put her head down (a helmet might have been helpful) and charged forward, pushing, shoving, hopping, and apologizing as needed until she was finally within touching distance of Johnny Shim.

He was about to enter his math classroom. She'd caught him just in the nick of time.

Moni tapped him on the shoulder. Well, maybe it was more like a gentle smack. Okay, she practically fell into him, but she was out of breath and exhausted from her harrowing journey.

"Ahh!" Johnny yelped, and turned around. She had startled him. Possibly terrified him.

"Ahh!" she exclaimed in return. Sometimes when other people screamed in your face the only thing to do was to scream right back.

"I'm very jumpy on Tuesdays!" he said, still a little wild-eyed. She noticed his hand over his heart. Good reminder. She stole a look down.

Dark, doomy blue. Ugh.

Johnny waited for Moni to speak. Or possibly to explain why she'd nearly attacked him outside of room 201 at 9:34 on a Tuesday morning.

Moni had forgotten to plan this part of the plan. So, naturally, she did what she always did when she was within touching distance of Johnny Shim with not a clue of what to say.

One . . . two . . . three . . .

"Are you counting something?" Johnny asked.

Moni had been mouthing the numbers.

Johnny turned to go into class. Desperately, Moni managed to call out, "Happy Tuesday!"

Well, that was a mega fail, Moni thought as she turned to go. Eco science was going to have to be extra eco-y to lift the funk she felt descending. *Stupid blue necklace*, she thought, moving to hide the charm underneath the collar of her T-shirt.

That's when she saw it: To her utter surprise, the charm at the top of the sparkling silver key radiated an exhilarating, icy blue.

So, Johnny Shim, gentle, sweet, jumpy Johnny Shim liked to be scared after all. Okay, she could work with that, no problem. She'd just have to get her prank on.

Chapter twelve

Later that week during gym class, another textbook Crush Necklace opportunity presented itself.

"We're doing baseline fitness tests for the next couple weeks," Coach Stoop announced. "Play hard. Play fair. Let your dreams begin and end right here in this gym. Your future starts now. Today is the day. Who is ready for this?"

"Woo!" Alex called out from behind her. Alex thought he was way better at general athletics than he actually was.

"Coach Stoop has got to get a grip," the girl sitting next to Moni muttered as she picked blue nail polish off her thumb.

Grace was out sick that day. Or more accurately out because "I could be getting a stuffy nose." Grace was good at faking an almost sickness when she needed to. Which on that particular day was too bad, because Coach Stoop was really on a roll, and if there's one thing the two best friends could easily crack jokes about, it was Coach Stoop's antics.

Coach Stoop still expected to be an Olympian one day. Though he was very nice for a middle-aged gym teacher with veiny legs and a mild but constant body odor, it was completely unclear to Moni how he'd gotten a job teaching *physical* education.

"This infamous fitness test includes—drumroll, please . . ." Coach Stoop insisted. Moni played along, lightly tapping her feet against the gym floor. Good thing they didn't have Friday Night Skate in there. The gym was old, and the wooden planks were neither smooth nor even. It would be a disaster to skate on such a surface. A massacre, really!

After a few more minutes of theatrics, Coach Stoop finally described the exercises to come. Today was Phase One, as he put it: push-ups and sit-ups.

"What brave ones would like to go in the first round?"

Nobody spoke. Or moved. Except for the girl next to Moni, who now worked on chipping the nail polish from her pinkie.

Moni really hated an awkward silence. "I'll do it,"

she announced, rising to her feet and stepping forward off the bleachers.

Alex jumped up right behind her. Of course. "Y'all ready for this gun show?" he said, turning in a full circle, flexing his stringy muscles.

"I'll go, too," Johnny said, bopping to the gym floor, joining Moni and Alex before the class.

What luck!

Moni noticed a flicker of blue neon at the bottom of her vision but didn't dare check. The rest of her class, and potentially Johnny, might catch her. She didn't want to be the weird girl staring at jewelry around her neck all the time. Dangly jewelry probably wasn't allowed in gym class, either, though there was a 99.99 percent chance Coach Stoop was too checked out to notice.

It took at least another eight minutes for Coach Stoop to convince eight more students to participate in round one. When it was finally time to get started, Moni made sure to secure a push-up spot on the floor right next to Johnny Shim. Unfortunately, Alex plopped down on her other side.

"On my count! Push-ups!" Coach Stoop roared. "Three . . . two . . . one . . . go!"

Sandwiched between the two boys, Moni executed as many push-ups as she possibly could. Alex dropped out early, claiming something he called "old runner's arm" in his biceps (yeah, right). Moni kept going. When her arms felt like straw, she did another. When they felt like al dente fettuccine, she did another. When they felt like electric-green sour straw candies, she collapsed onto her stomach.

"Never. Moving. Again," Moni panted. "Bring. Popsicles. ASAP." She thought she heard Johnny chuckle.

Johnny managed to pull off five more push-ups before he crumbled to the ground next to her. His crash down reminded Moni to check her necklace.

Bright, bright blue.

She thought about what Raya had said the other day. *Boys are babies and can't handle losing*, or something like that. Hmm. Maybe Raya was right, both about boys and Moni not trusting her intuition. Never in a million years would she have expected the necklace to turn bright blue after Johnny became runner-up in Phase One of the baseline test.

* * *

At lunchtime, Moni texted Grace. Moni saw Harley and Raya perched at the Music Box Steps, but didn't have the courage to approach them without her best friend. She scuttled to a quiet spot behind the oak tree with the roots that looked like a sea creature. It felt kind of nice to be alone.

Necklace is on fiiiiiirrrreeee, Moni typed.

Immediately, Grace responded: Tell me.

Moni explained what went down in PE. Grace responded after a few minutes with a cartwheel emoji, a thumbs-up emoji, and an exclamation point.

Coach Stoop is nuts. You woulda died.

I bet, Grace replied.

I think I'm on a roll here! This Crush Necklace is the best! I have soooo many more ideas for special op plans!

Grace didn't respond right away. Moni leaned back against the tree and replayed the gym class triumph in her head.

She checked her phone. Maybe she had missed an incoming message. Nothing.

After a few minutes, a bubble appeared, indicating Grace was typing, but then it disappeared.

Finally, with only a few minutes left before the next period, Moni's phone buzzed.

Awesome was all Grace's text said. Then, Gonna nap, feel like barf.

Shoot, Moni had completely forgotten the real reason why Grace wasn't in class in the first place.

OMG sorry forgot to ask! You feeling ok?

Bad bad bad, Grace typed.

Feel better!!!!!

K thx

Moni put her phone in her back pocket and headed to history class. K thx, no period, no exclamation point. Seemed a little cold, but Moni shrugged it off. Grace was sick, that's all. Nothing to read into . . . right?

Chapter Thirteen

Over the next week, Moni continued to seize all opportunities to collect crush evidence from Johnny Shim using her necklace. And most of those opportunities came in the form of trying to get really close to Johnny Shim in a non-creepy way and then seeing if her necklace changed colors. Needless to say, this approach had led to many an awkward run-in that left Moni frustrated.

But as far as Moni was concerned, there was no time to waste. As Harley and Raya kept reminding her, the next Friday Night Skate was a little over two weeks away. Naively, Moni had always thought Friday Night Skate was literally just an excuse to dress up, roller skate with friends, and maybe indulge in a couple Dixie cups of stale pretzels. She'd been wrong. As Harley and Raya continued to emphasize, the fate of a crush could live and die at Friday Night Skate, especially if a stairwell opportunity went awry. Moni nodded like she understood, though what on Earth could go so wrong in that musty, concrete stairwell behind the snack bar, Moni had no clue. But Harley and Raya had yet to steer her off course, and she still had her handy Crush Necklace. For now, Moni tried to focus on figuring out how to keep her Crush Necklace bright blue.

Simple as that, she kept reminding herself.

Especially if she stuck to a strategy already proven to be effective: sneaking up behind Johnny Shim and startling him. She waited until the next Tuesday because (Moni had been listening) Johnny Shim was jumpy on Tuesdays.

Also, the cafeteria served pizza on Tuesdays. Double win.

That Tuesday, rain poured relentlessly from the sky, so Mason Mill Middle School students were all cooped up inside the cafeteria during lunch. Moni sat with Harley, Raya, and Grace at a table near the windows. Harley and Raya frantically tried to finish their homework for their afternoon classes while they munched on candy corn and Swedish Fish (brain food, they both insisted), and Grace scrolled through photos on her phone. Moni played with the pizza crusts on her tray. It wasn't the most social lunch.

"You going to eat those?" Moni asked when she noticed Grace had picked all the pepperoni off her slice.

"Ew, no," she answered, wrinkling her nose. Moni swooped them up. Pepperoni was delicious. Since when did Grace not like the sumptuous disks of pure yum?

"Take mine, too," Harley said, pushing her tray across the table. "I'm weaning off processed meat."

"My pleasure." Moni reached to pluck the pepperoni from Harley's plate, when she saw Johnny Shim saunter into the cafeteria and get on line for food. This was Moni's chance.

"Be right back," she said, grabbing two greasy pepperonis and jetting across the room in Johnny's direction.

Prowling forward sneakily, Moni arrived within touching distance of Johnny just as he received his lunch. She saw, quietly peering over his shoulder, a lukewarm slice of pepperoni on his tray. Sweet, he liked pepperoni, too!

Go time.

As Johnny turned toward Moni, she threw the pepperoni she'd rescued from Harley's plate over her eyes, opened her arms big and wide, and delivered her line (she'd come prepared this time). "Pepperoni Tuesday Monster!" Moni yelled.

Johnny didn't yell back this time. Instead, she heard his tray crash to the floor.

Success!

The pepperoni covering her right eye fell to the floor, making a soft *splat*. Moni blinked to clear the lingering grease from her eyelashes. She noticed the confusion on Johnny's face.

"Scare ya?" Moni asked excitedly, pulling a pepperoni off her left eye. Johnny's mouth hung agape, and his shoulders appeared tense. Yup, she'd definitely startled him.

Frantically, she checked her necklace. An Arctic blue. Uh-oh.

"I told you. I'm very, very jumpy," he spat.

With that, Johnny Shim picked his food up off the ground and stormed out of the cafeteria. Moni stood, wiping pepperoni grease off her eyes, feeling like a fool. A confused, blue-necklaced fool.

Chapter Fourteen

Moni thought about the botched pizza scare for a couple days before coming to the obvious conclusion: She'd gotten too excited. Or, rather, failed to conceal her excitement. She'd broken rule number one. Of *course* the Crush Necklace hadn't turned bright blue. Duh.

So Moni's next genius plan, the trusty mini-marshmallow-rocket-ship sneak attack, was born.

Moni's confidence remained a bit shaken, so she recruited Grace to help with the operation. She wouldn't make the same mistake again. No matter what, she would harness her enthusiasm. Grace had complained that she didn't like the idea of performing the trick in front of an audience, but when Moni promised she could keep the bag of mini marshmallows after the mission was complete, she agreed to help.

Moni and Grace's mini marshmallow obsession

began when they were in third grade, a year after officially becoming best friends. It was only natural that they began training in the fine athletic art of throwing mini marshmallows into each other's mouths from a distance. Years later, Grace was the designated thrower, Moni the official marshmallow-in-mouth catcher. Their record was the length of Moni's hallway, which as it turned out was nearly fifteen feet.

The mini-marshmallow-rocket-ship sneak attack took place right after the last bell, as Johnny collected his books from his locker. Moni hadn't even needed Raya's spy work to learn his locker number; she'd figured that one out all on her own on the first few days of school. Armed with a fresh bag of the fluffy, sugary snack, the girls approached.

Go time.

"Incoming!" Grace called as she expertly launched a mini marshmallow toward Johnny Shim's locker.

"I got it, I got it," Moni yelled, careful to remain aware of both her proximity to Johnny Shim and the tiny marshmallow as she motioned for the other kids in the hallway to make room.

Grace's high-arching throw was perfect. Moni

caught the mini marshmallow in her mouth, just inches in front of Johnny Shim, no problem.

"Victory!" Moni exclaimed, throwing her arms over her head and gently bumping her back into Johnny's shoulder. "Oh, sorry. Didn't see you there," she said casually.

"We still got it!" Grace cheered from down the hallway.

"Very impressive" was all Johnny said. But he smiled big when he said it.

Moni shrugged. It took all of her self-control not to dissolve into her toothiest smile. "No biggie," she replied nonchalantly. With that, she turned on her heel and walked down the hall to where Grace waited.

Grace confirmed with a nod that the necklace was indeed bright blue. Everything had gone exactly as planned. Then why did Moni suddenly feel less than victorious?

"Nice party trick," Alex said as he walked by holding his hand up for a high five. Indulging him, Grace raised her hand to slap his. If Moni had been paying attention, she would have seen that Grace's cheeks bloomed deep, spunky pink nearly as bright as the blue of the Crush Necklace.

Chapter Fifteen

Despite the nagging feeling in the pit of her stomach, Moni was ultimately encouraged by the mini marshmallow victory to try something riskier. More personal. More private. She felt it was time to take things back to the roots. Or rocks, rather.

Moni announced her plan to the group text the following week.

Got something extra great for Johnny!

Rad, Harley responded a few minutes later.

I HATE ECO SCIENCE WITH A BURNING PASSION!! Raya contributed.

Moni, who'd finished their big science assignment the night before, couldn't take her mind away from her brilliant plan.

Don't want to spill the beans, but it involves . . . wait for it . . . props!!!

Props are fun, Raya added.

Grace only replied hours later: Kewl

No period. No exclamation point. But Moni hardly noticed. She was busy making sure all of the Crush Necklace entries in her fun fact journal were accurate and up-to-date.

That weekend, Moni made a solo trip to Bell Lake. Officially closed for the season, the beachfront was nearly empty. Moni took her time collecting as many peanut butter cup–sized rocks as she could find. She'd left her phone at home, so it was just her, the dirt-sand, the lake, and the early fall breeze. It was both a peaceful and productive afternoon; Moni left with a total of twelve paintable rocks in her tote.

She'd initially planned to present her gift on Wednesday—something to look forward to in the middle of the week, but on Monday she was so excited she couldn't wait. Not that she would let Johnny Shim (or anyone, for that matter) see her enthusiasm. No way. She marched to school that morning with a mini-mart bag of special lake rocks in her backpack and a determined bounce in her step.

In case the rock presentation went over well, Moni also brought with her a baggie of Popsicle sticks as a potential bonus. She'd scrounged enough couch change to buy a box of rainbow Popsicles. It had been her absolute pleasure to eat all but one in the box while her mom was at work the evening before. Moni had washed the Popsicle sticks with soap and drizzled them with boiling water from the kettle to try to get the faint stain of artificial flavoring out.

Before school Monday morning, Johnny Shim stood near the Music Box Steps, laughing about something or another with two friends. Both of his companions wore oversized headphones around their necks and pants that could certainly benefit from belts. Their appearance made Moni appreciate Johnny's purple Converse even more. His two friends must have been eighth graders. Moni didn't recognize them. At least they all seemed to be enjoying themselves. Best to catch Johnny Shim when in a good mood, she reasoned.

Moni marched right up and deliberately tapped him on the shoulder. When he turned around, he looked happy to see her . . . at least, she thought he did.

"I thought you could use these," she said, handing him the baggie and dangling it playfully before him.

Johnny looked at her quizzically. Moni noticed the headphone boys turn to face her as well, as if they were part of the exchange. Which they clearly weren't. Maybe approaching him mid-conversation with his slightly intimidating friends wasn't the best idea.

Could her Crush Necklace be turning bright blue anyway? She was too nervous to check just yet. If she broke eye contact with Johnny Shim, she feared he might float away, never to return.

She gave the baggie another little shake.

"You know, for your dreams?" she clarified.

"I know," he snapped in a hushed voice. It was possible that the sound Headphone Boy #1 made was a snicker.

Moni was doing it again: *one . . . two . . . three . . .* That's when she noticed Johnny's cheeks start to blush. Unlike some people who smile or look down or dig their toe in the dirt when they blush, Johnny Shim's mouth became very tight. His lips nearly disappeared. She'd never seen him like that before.

Moni had to do something. Covering it with an

extra big blink, Moni checked her necklace. Darkest, doomiest blue.

"I know these are a little different than your usual rocks, but will they work?" she asked. This plan had to succeed. He loved painting rocks, right? That was, like, one of their things!

Johnny Shim nodded in response. He made no move to take the baggie from her outstretched hand.

"Dude, come listen to this remix," Headphone Boy #1 said, presumably queuing up a song on his phone.

"Swag," Headphones Boy #2 said in a way that somehow made his acne more pronounced.

Moni was so very glad Johnny Shim was nothing like those boys.

"Yup, yup," he answered over his shoulder in a voice a few pitches deeper than his usual tone.

Johnny Shim turned back to Moni. "That was very considerate." Swoon. Moni loved it when he used polysyllabic words. If her Crush Necklace worked in reverse, indicating her own emotion, it would have burned a blinding blue.

"What do you keep looking down at, by the way?" Shoot. He'd caught her.

"Uh . . ." Moni had to think fast. "I heard a rumor

that it's good to look down when you blink to clear sun particles from your eyeballs. It's, like, a science thing."

Johnny smiled, then laughed.

"That's completely ridiculous, Moni Hayes," he said. Finally, he took the bag. "Thanks."

To Moni, Johnny Shim's laugh was better than all the Crush Necklaces in the world. Still, she checked the charm hanging around her neck. Finally, radiant blue. Moni had triumphed after all.

Johnny turned back around to join whatever dumb thing the two headphones boys were talking about or listening to.

"Who's your rock friend?" she heard one of them ask in a way that made it seem like he equated rocks to Legos or action figures or something for little kids.

"Nobody," Johnny said quickly. "I mean, nothing. I mean, swag."

Maybe Johnny Shim was like those boys.

Moni checked her necklace again. Still bright blue, though her own heart sank. Johnny didn't introduce her to his friends, which wasn't good manners at all. Was she embarrassing? Annoying? Horrible? Monstrous? Or worse, really just nobody?

No. Her necklace was bright blue. Thank goodness for her necklace. She made a fist around the charm with her right hand as she walked away, Popsicle sticks burning a hole in the back pocket of her jeans.

Moni ran into Grace as she approached the steps that led to the school's entrance. To her surprise, Alex walked alongside her.

"Just talking about homework stuff!" Grace declared when she saw the confused look on Moni's face. "See ya, Alex!"

Alex smiled his metal smile, gave Grace a fist bump, and faded into the crowd.

"That was confusing," Moni said, reflecting on the rock encounter, though the Alex interaction was equally bizarre now that she thought about it.

"What isn't?" Grace mumbled. She didn't ask any more questions, though, which Moni found slightly disappointing.

Chapter Sixteen

The next day, Coach Stoop was nothing short of geared up for Phase Two of the baseline fitness test. Maybe it was that they got to go outside in order to use the track, and the change of scenery was enough to make his day. Coach Stoop's day, to be exact.

"Today is the dreaded one-mile run," Coach Stoop said. Some people groaned. Moni and Grace shared a smile because Coach Stoop spoke as if he were telling a ghost story. It was one of his most outrageous qualities. "One of the more challenging athletic tests. Remember: Be strategic, be strong, and push through cramps, fatigue, and any sudden-onset hiccups."

"Hiccups?" Moni whispered to Grace.

"He's actually insane," she said with an eye roll.

When the class scattered around the track to stretch, Moni kept an eye on Johnny Shim.

"Do you think Johnny is faster than me?" Moni asked Grace as she leaned over to touch her toes.

"Doubtful," Grace replied.

"I think this is a really good Crush Necklace opportunity."

"Isn't it always?"

"Not *always*," Moni said, deaf to Grace's sarcasm. "I think the mile is great because we'll be held captive on the track. As long as I can keep up with him." Grace stood on one leg, stretching her quad. "I'll call this the Catch Me If You Can Plan."

Turned out that wasn't the most accurate title. Moni had no problem catching up to Johnny, but she did have trouble staying with him.

They were no more than 100 meters into the run and Johnny (mimicked by Moni) had fallen to the back of the pack. And then ten paces behind the back of the pack. And then closer to twenty. After the first of the four loops, Moni feared Grace or one of the other front-runners would lap them before the mile was even over. For a moment, Moni wondered if she could speed walk at the same pace of their slug-gish jog. She'd never been a sprinter, exactly, but she'd gotten caught in enough thunderstorms with Grace on the way home from Tina's Treasures to build a natural endurance. It appeared the same was not the case for Johnny Shim.

"You can speed up if you want," Johnny said between pants. They were two laps in, and Moni's necklace remained a dark navy.

"Oh, it's okay," Moni said, pretending to be out of breath. "I don't think I'll last if I go faster."

It was kind of fun being alone with Johnny on the track. Or, at least, away from the commotion of their classmates. Was this a date?

"So . . . come here often?" she joked.

Johnny shook his head. She noticed his cheeks were flushed bright pink.

All in all it was a very awkward and a very slow mile. Moni made sure he crossed the finish line exactly one step before her. The necklace hadn't turned bright blue once, and Moni had remembered to check every ten steps.

Moni was confused. Had she read the signs wrong? When she lost the push-up test, the necklace turned bright blue without hesitation. Why didn't it work when he beat her in the mile? Should she have lost by more? Without walking, that would have been practically impossible.

"Okay," Coach Scoot said as he marked down their times. And then to Moni directly, "Next time I hope you try your best."

"That was kind of desperate," Grace said during their cool-down stretches.

Moni checked her necklace as Johnny walked by on his way to get water.

"Don't worry, Moni. Your necklace didn't fly off or anything," Johnny said. "It's not like we were running *that* fast."

Moni was stunned. Johnny could be mean. But mostly, that was the first time she could recall him calling her by her first name alone.

Johnny Shim and her Crush Necklace were both riddles that Moni was seemingly incapable of solving.

Chapter Seventeen

On Wednesday, Grace and Moni walked home from school. Soccer practice had been canceled on account of a muddy field. The home opener was the next day and something about not wanting to tear up the pitch before the first game of the season.

"So what do you think is a good strategy I can try tomorrow? I've really diversified my efforts, and this crazy necklace is just so unpredictable!" Moni complained. "Or should I say, Johnny Shim is unpredictable. Duh."

"I'm kind of nervous about this game coming up."

"Why? You're going to kill it, you always do," Moni said, but Grace didn't respond. "So I was thinking of going big with the Mega Poppy Seed Test. MPST, that's what I'm calling it. I told you about that, right?"

"Maybe," Grace said. "I don't know."

"Yeah, I think MPST is the way to go. I mean, you

said the necklace was bright blue at the lake when you called out that poppy seed in my teeth situation, right?" Moni felt suddenly panicked. If that hadn't been true, then her whole plan would be completely shot. She'd have to start from scratch, go back to the drawing board.

"Yup, it was bright blue," Grace said as she kicked a rock off the sidewalk.

"Ooh, is that a flat one? I think Johnny likes the flat ones." Moni scrambled to look at the stone. "You know, to paint his . . . never mind." She'd learned her lesson about talking about Johnny's dream rocks in front of others.

"Right. So, yeah, I think the game tomorrow is going to be a really big deal. Like kind of seals my fate for the future, or something."

"Really?"

"Yup."

"That's a lot of pressure, Grace. It can't possibly."

"Yeah, actually, I think it does. Our coach talks to the high school varsity coach, you know," Grace snapped. "The varsity coach is coming to scout."

"I didn't know," Moni shot back defensively. Then, quietly, "Sorry. I didn't know."

Grace kicked another rock.

"I'll be there tomorrow to cheer you on. Don't worry," Moni offered, putting her arm around her taller and apparently more nervous best friend.

"Okay. Thanks."

"Don't mention it," Moni answered, relieved their momentary tiff seemed to be extinguished. "Ooh! Maybe Johnny Shim will be there, too!"

"Goodie," Grace said flatly.

"Anyway, we should hustle," Moni said. "That show about people making their swimming pools fancier on a budget comes on in five."

"Actually, I think I'm just going to go home."

"Really?" That was unlike Grace. They always watched silly TV after school. Well, before soccer had taken over and dominated so much free time. Grace especially loved any renovation show involving a swimming pool.

"Yeah. I just kinda want to chill."

"Okay, sure," Moni said, forcing the pep to remain in her voice. "We'll just watch another time. No big deal. Next time you don't have practice."

The girls walked two more blocks together in silence before they arrived at Moni's apartment complex. They hugged goodbye, like they always did, but Moni was afraid to look her best friend in the eye. She wondered if Grace felt the same way. Moni kicked a rock on her way across the parking lot to her apartment entrance. The same toe she had used to incorrectly kick the soccer ball on lake day throbbed.

Moni had mostly forgotten about her strange walk with Grace by the time her mom got home that night. She'd already finished all her homework and was busy updating her Crush Necklace slash fun fact journal on the floor in front of the TV, when her mom walked in the door and collapsed onto the couch.

"I. Am. So. Tired," she moaned. "Pizza?"

"Meat lovers special?"

"Meat lovers special, double meat," Moni's mom answered. Which was actually code for plain cheese.

Moni's phone buzzed.

"You've been blowing up all week, Love Straw," Moni's mom observed.

"Oh, just the girls," Moni said absently as she rapidly typed in her response. Harley was asking which TV show to watch next, and Moni was trying to get everyone on board with this cartoon about chemistry that she knew sounded really boring and lame but was actually really funny and informative.

"All right, I'm ordering the pizza plus two cherry Cokes, because sometimes you just gotta treat yo' self."

MPST tomorrow. Stay tuned!! Moni typed to the group, now that she was at it.

"Fun fact time, before I turn into an official zombie," Moni's mom said from the couch. Moni locked her phone, tossed it aside, and paged through her notebook.

"Let's see. Johnny Shim made my necklace—" Moni stopped herself short and scrambled to rephrase. She didn't like keeping secrets from her mom, but the necklace was hers and Grace's alone. Maybe Johnny Shim's, too, if you wanted to get conceptual about it. She started again. "Johnny Shim found the mini-marshmallow-rocket-ship sneak attack very impressive, which did not surprise me."

"Hmmm," Moni's mom hummed, eyes already closed. "You're paying a lot of attention to this Johnny Shim."

"I have a secret weapon," Moni said after a beat. "A compass."

"Okay, Love Straw. Well, he'd be a fool not to like you inside and out. In an age-appropriate kind of way, that is."

"Yes, Mom, don't worry."

"That's my Love Straw."

Moni's mom was asleep before the pizza arrived.

Chapter Eighteen

Moni knew the Mega Poppy Seed Test was borderline desperate. And also maybe borderline crazy. But she *was* desperate and starting to feel as if she were going crazy. Plus, she loved poppy seed bagels.

It was a beautiful day, so the girls, along with most of the middle school, sat around the concrete court-yard outside the cafeteria during lunch. Moni had woken up extra early to stop by the diner on the way to school to pick up the bagels. "Y'all heard the Friday Night Skate theme, right?" Harley asked the group while she texted. Moni chomped on her second poppy seed bagel. Delicious. "Not impressed."

"Pshhh, you and me both," Raya said as she crunched on a salt-and-vinegar potato chip.

"What is it?" Moni couldn't believe another skate was just one day away. *Time flies when you're busy Crush Necklacing!* she thought.

"Under the Sea," Grace confirmed, without looking up from her phone. "I heard Alex say he's going to dress up as a submarine."

Under the Sea. That was, well, an absolutely fantastic theme. Practically limitless! Moni's mind reeled with ideas for costumes: mermaid . . . merman . . . shark . . . octopus . . . seahorse . . . sea foam (maybe not) . . . shipwreck . . . clam . . . The list could go on.

"Tina's after my game today?" Grace asked quietly, just to Moni.

"Duh," Moni replied as she pulled out her cell phone to use the reverse camera screen as a mirror. Perfect. About 60 percent of the cracks between her teeth were filled with poppy seeds, like a log overcrowded with ants. "Be right back," she announced to the group, before jumping to her feet and bouncing over to where Johnny sat on the opposite side of the courtyard. He was alone, knees tucked up to his chest, doodling in a notebook.

When Moni was within touching distance, she said, "So, Friday Night Skate is tomorrow." She smiled extra big.

Johnny looked up, nodded, and returned to his drawing.

Moni checked her necklace.

"Are you excited?"

"I guess," Johnny said without shifting his gaze.

Moni checked her necklace.

"I am. I think it's going to be so fun."

Johnny nodded again, eyes glued to the page. Moni checked her necklace and kept the smile plastered to her face, even though she felt anything but happy. How could she get him to look up and notice the poppy seeds?

"Selfie!" Moni declared. She pulled out her phone and crouched next to Johnny Shim for an impromptu photo op. Her phone screen reflected their faces like a grainy mirror. Johnny Shim couldn't miss her poppy seed smile now!

Before Moni could snap the picture, Johnny Shim squirmed away.

"Hey, I'm not really in the mood for selfies or company right now," he said, pulling his knees closer to his chest.

Moni stood back up and checked her necklace, both to see its color and to keep from bursting into tears.

A depressing blue.

"Sorry," she said, retreating as quickly as possible.

For a moment, Moni hated her necklace. She hated Johnny's stupid doodle notebook, dream rocks, and pepperoni. And she anything but hated Johnny Shim. Because even though he had hurt her feelings and made her feel like a fool, she totally understood the need to be alone.

Alex stood reading something over Grace's shoulder when Moni returned. Why was Alex always popping up out of nowhere? Moni gave him a limp wave and a half smile as a greeting. Even though her heart felt bruised, she still had good manners.

"Yo, Moni, you have, like, a whole ecosystem in your teeth." Polysyllabic words from Alex's mouth were in no way swoonable.

"You're one to talk!" she retorted. Alex shrugged and bounced away.

Moni slunk back to her seat at the end of the table. Harley and Grace sat close together, whispering about something. The thought that they might be talking about her briefly crossed Moni's mind.

"You have at least fifty-two thousand poppy seeds in your teeth, Monilee," Raya observed. "But If you help me finish this stupid science worksheet, I'll pretend it's your new lewk."

Moni sighed, attempting to dislodge any of the tiny seeds with her tongue. By the end of lunch, the worksheet was done and Raya confirmed only 11,000 poppy seeds remained. Moni still felt like a bit of a fool.

"Thanks for the help, Monilee." Moni felt a small swell of pride. It was nice to receive a compliment without feeling the impulse to confirm its effect on a dumb old necklace. "Oh, and as for Johnny 'Purple Shoes' Shim, I'm going to do you a solid and enlist Tati at Friday Night Skate. You're welcome."

Great. Another force working on Moni's behalf in efforts to win Johnny Shim's affection. Just what Moni needed.

· She spent the rest of the day rescuing captive poppy seeds from among her molars.

Chapter Nineteen

When it was time for the girls' home opening soccer game, Moni was glad the role of spectator extraordinaire required minimal physical exertion. Between the low-key hallway stalking, the rock escapade, the baseline tests, and waking up early for the poppy seed bagels that morning, Moni was exhausted. Not just physically, but her mind was fried. It wasn't that she was ungrateful that the Crush Necklace was bestowed upon her by the powers of the universe, but between conjuring up numerous plans to execute, checking in with the necklace, obsessing over what Johnny Shim was or was not responding to, documenting the positive results in her journal, and then relaying almost all of that info to Harley, Raya, and Grace . . . well, Moni Hayes was pooped.

But not too pooped to cheer on her friends.

Moni was going to applaud when the Mason Mill Mustangs scored. Moni was going to shout at the ref if he made a bad call. Moni was going to wave her signs for anyone and everyone to see. In short, Moni was going to have fun, whether her Crush Necklace liked it or not.

She didn't mention it to Grace because she wanted it to be a surprise, but she'd stayed up late the night before making big, colorful posters to bring to the game. Moni had brought four so she could rotate throughout the game. Written in big, bold letters, complete with decorative soccer balls, suns, stick figure horses (not the easiest mascot to illustrate), and zigzags, the signs really were a showstopper, as far as Moni was concerned. They almost rivaled the costumes she'd assembled for the first Friday Night Skate.

When Moni arrived at the field, she took a seat in the front row. She'd made sure to get there a few minutes early, in case the game was packed. It wasn't. But it was a beautiful early fall afternoon, not a cloud in the sky. Perfect spectating weather.

The Mason Mill Mustangs looked dynamite when they took the field in their fresh forest green uniforms. The visiting team didn't stand a chance. Especially with Grace starting at right wing. Moni spotted Raya in the center of the field and Harley holding it down behind her on defense. As the two teams waited for the referee to blow the whistle for kickoff, Grace hopped in place. Moni couldn't tell if she was warming up or if she was bouncing to calm her nerves. Maybe both.

"Let's go, Mustangs!" Moni cheered. She had plenty of room around her in the stands to raise and wave her signs with reckless abandon. *Grace got goalzzz!!* was her favorite, though *I get a _kick_ out of you, G-$*, *#9 you're kickin' fine*, and *Mustangs for president(s)!* were nothing to frown at.

The ball bounced around for the first few minutes of the game. Moni screamed her butt off whenever the ball neared Grace. Grace's lanky body appeared a little jumbled, like she didn't quite know how to move her legs and arms at the same time, but every time she got the ball, her body responded as if on instinct. Moni heard footsteps on the metal bleachers coming from behind her but didn't turn to look. Her gaze was fixed on her best friend.

"Sorry I was so rude at lunch," Johnny said, as if

picking up from where they'd last left off. It startled Moni when he did this, but she also kind of liked it. It was efficient.

"Oh, it's okay," Moni said, even though the memory of the encounter still burned.

"I've had a bad day. Rough couple of days, actually."

"I get it," Moni said, even though she wasn't sure if she did.

"I am excited about Friday Night Skate. I have a really rad costume idea, I think," he offered.

Moni quickly checked her charm. Still dark blue, but her gut told her sparks of bright blue were soon to ignite.

"That's awesome," Moni said. "Costumes are the best."

"I agree, Moni Hayes. And so are your signs. These must have taken forever to make."

"Nah. Just forever minus an hour."

"Really good signs."

"Thanks, I . . ." Moni tried to think of a joke, but instead opted for the simple truth. "Came up with them myself."

"Something from nothing."

"Kind of."

"May I?" he asked, pointing toward the extra posters leaning against their seats.

"Why don't you take these two?" Moni said, handing him the *Grace got goalzzz!!* and *Mustangs for president(s)!* signs. "You can alternate."

Just then Raya kicked a ball upfield and Grace launched herself after it, saving it just before it rolled out of bounds.

"You're an animal, Grace!" Moni screamed at the top of her lungs. "Number nine all the time!"

It felt great to yell, sometimes.

"You should try it," she said to Johnny.

"Soccer?"

"No," she said with a laugh. "This . . ." Moni paused to take a big breath in. "Grace for governor!"

"Ooh, I see," Johnny said with a serious nod. "Will this do?" Johnny took a deep breath and bellowed, "Mustangs to the moon!"

Moni, not one to be upstaged, jumped to her feet and repeated his borderline nonsensical cheer with gusto.

"Mustangs to the mooooooon!" they screamed together, holding the double *o* in *moon* until their lungs were empty.

"You're fun, Moni Hayes," he said.

Moni smiled. She remembered one of Raya's instructions. *Boys love it when you're having fun.* Moni looked down at her necklace and wasn't surprised one bit when she saw the charm was exactly the color she'd hoped.

Moni and Johnny watched the rest of the game together. Or, rather, they sat together chatting the rest of the game. When Grace got the ball near the sideline, Moni made sure to cheer as loud as possible. At halftime, the score was 1–1, though Moni couldn't recall exactly when or how the goals had taken place. At the start of the second half, Johnny left to go to the restroom and returned with two sodas.

"Hope you like cherry Coke," he said, handing her the can.

"Duh. Most sophisticated kind of Coke out there," she said, popping the tab, noticing that her necklace remained the brightest of blues.

Moni took a big swig of her drink.

"You must really like that necklace," Johnny commented.

Soda almost erupted out of Moni's nose.

"What do you mean? It's all right. I like it a totally

normal amount, I think." Moni was suddenly very self-conscious.

"It's just that ever since you started wearing it, you are constantly looking at it. Like it's about to escape or something."

"Oh." Moni tucked the charm underneath her T-shirt. "Habits."

Though, now that she sat next to Johnny Shim, drinking a delicious cherry Coke and cheering on her best friend with top-notch homemade signs, she wondered if she even needed the necklace at all. For the first time since she started seventh grade, everything seemed just right.

Moni and Johnny talked nonstop during the second half of the game. He told her about Portland, Maine (not Oregon), and how the leaves looked like a bonfire this time of year. He said that he missed his old friends and the shore near where he grew up because it had the best rocks. He revealed that his older brother, Calvin, wasn't as bad as their mom thought, even though he generally gave terrible advice. Calvin and his parents fought a lot, and it made Johnny's ears hurt sometimes. The brothers were nothing alike; Johnny considered himself an old soul while he was convinced Calvin could never mature beyond the temperament of a toddler. Every now and then Moni noticed that the Mustangs' offense got the ball, and she'd yell, "To the goal, Grace!" or "Nice play, number nine!" toward the field. But mostly Moni listened to Johnny with her ears and her eyes. So much so that the action of the soccer game faded into the background.

We are here, Moni thought. *We are right here.*

During the second half of the game, she didn't check her necklace once.

The Mason Mill Mustangs won 2–1. After the final whistle and the obligatory handshakes, Moni took her signs and ran onto the field to congratulate Grace.

"Victory!" she exclaimed, nearly tackling her friend. "We won!"

Grace shrugged her off. Moni persisted.

"You were awesome! You played so well!"

Grace remained silent. Moni tried again.

"And I'm pretty positive all my awesome signs totally distracted the other team." Moni wiggled *Grace got goalzzz!!* in front of her. She was surprised

Grace hadn't commented on them immediately. It was truly some of her best handiwork yet.

"Or totally embarrassed me, either way."

Moni felt a little ping in her chest. Ouch.

"Well, I thought you played really well. I'm sure you impressed that varsity coach you were talking about."

"Moni, I was subbed off. Half the time you were cheering for me, I wasn't even on the field."

Moni scrambled to cover her tracks. Truthfully, she hadn't noticed. "Yeah, but before that."

"I was taken out before the end of the first half. Nobody is subbed off in the first half! I played horribly! Anyone with half a brain could see that!" Grace's face was flushed. "Which you probably couldn't because you are so obsessed with Johnny Shim! He's, like, all you can pay attention to these days."

"That's not true," Moni argued.

"Give me a break. 'OMG, is my necklace bright blue?'" Grace mocked. Another ping. Ouch. "Literally, that's all you talk about. You're not even yourself. Ever since you got that stupid magic necklace, your crush on him is all you care about."

Grace stormed away.

"Grace, I—"

But it was no use; Grace had already disappeared into a crowd of people, and Moni figured this wasn't the right time to push her best friend. Had Grace been right? Had Moni become so obsessed with Johnny that she totally neglected what was going on in Grace's life? Moni sighed and turned to walk away, but when she did, her jaw dropped.

It was Johnny Shim. Within touching distance.

And he'd heard everything.

Chapter Twenty

Moni went straight home after her fight with Grace. She didn't have the strength to face Harley or Raya and definitely not Johnny Shim after what he'd witnessed. When she entered her empty apartment, she went directly into her room and slammed the door behind her. She proceeded to call and text Grace at least a dozen times, but got zero response. She considered texting Harley or Raya to see if everything was okay (which she knew it wasn't), but she thought better of it. Reaching out to Raya and or Harley about Grace would just start more drama. Would they pick sides? Moni assumed they would back Grace because of the whole soccer team thing. Would the group of friends dissolve? They were a group now, weren't they?

Despite her racing thoughts, Moni fell asleep face-down on her pillow, lights on, cell phone pressed against her cheek. It was dark out when her mom came in to wake her up for dinner.

"Hey, baby," Moni's mom whispered, gently brushing a piece of hair out of her daughter's eyes. "You hungry?"

Moni stretched and rolled over. Her cheeks were sticky, as if she'd been crying in her sleep. She kept her eyes tightly shut.

"Is it tomorrow yet?"

"Still tonight," Moni's mom said. "Everything okay, Love Straw?"

Moni held her breath to keep from talking and from crying.

"What's going on, Moni? Bad day?"

Moni opened her eyes. Her mom's tattoo came into focus. *Be yourself. Everyone else is taken.* She remembered the night of the first Friday Night Skate when Harley asked what the tattoo said.

Moni, suddenly, was furious.

"What's up, Moni?" her mom pressed.

"I don't have to tell you everything, okay! You're not a kid—you're still my mom!"

Moni's mom stiffened, and Moni immediately felt

ashamed. She'd never talked to her mom like that before.

"Dinner's ready" was all she said.

Moni shoved her phone into her pocket and followed behind her mom into the kitchen. Her mom still wore her uniform from work, which wasn't really a uniform so much as black pants, a black top, and bright red clogs. A little pop of color. She noticed a smear of either ketchup or syrup on her calf.

Two dishes of pasta sat on the kitchen table. Tiny tennis rackets under a snowy mound of Parmesan. The sight of the dinner made Moni want to cry for a reason she couldn't identify.

"Hydrate," her mom said, handing Moni a glass of hibiscus iced tea. They sat at the table and ate in silence. Moni speared one tennis racket at a time with her fork.

They'd never fought like this before. Moni was in fights with two people now, she realized. The two people she loved most.

Moni's pocket buzzed. It was a text to the group from Raya.

Tidal wave group lewk for FNS2 tomorrow. Easiest/ best costume ever!!

Moni noticed that this was a statement, not a question. From experience, Moni knew that usually the easiest costumes weren't the best, but whatever. It's not like she had a BFF to go shopping with and make a costume for anyway.

Rad! Harley responded.

A message from Grace popped up not a second after. You betcha!!! How could Grace send such an excited-sounding text given that they were in a potentially friendship-ending fight?

"I didn't think I'd ever have to say this, but no phones at the table? That's like a rule civilized people have, right?" There weren't a lot of rules in the Hayes household.

"I guess." Moni sighed. She responded to the group with a short K, locked the screen, and let the phone fall to the carpeted floor beneath her feet. She felt defeated.

"Fun fact?" Moni's mom asked after several more minutes of silent chewing.

Moni rolled her eyes. Nothing felt fun, and she hardly even knew what was true anymore.

"You first," Moni mumbled.

"Okay." Moni's mom proceeded without pause. "I never told you why I got this, did I?" Moni's mom asked, gesturing to the words etched into her forearm.

"No, but I'm sure Harley would be all ears," Moni shot back. She regretted it the second the words came out of her mouth.

"What is up with you, Moni Dylan? It's not like you to be so nasty."

"Maybe it is!" she argued, knowing deep down her mom was right. "I'm sorry. I had the worst day ever. I can't talk about it," Moni insisted, the backs of her eyeballs tingling—a sure sign of more tears.

"Well, I'm terribly sorry you had a bad day. I'm happy to listen if you want to talk, but I won't have this attitude. You're not acting like the kid I know."

Moni realized she didn't even know who that was anymore.

She groaned, exhausted. "I think I peaked in sixth grade," she admitted to her bowl of half-eaten tennis rackets. Moni saw what she thought was a hint of a smile creep at the edge of her mom's lips. She hadn't meant to be funny. "I'm serious."

"I know you are, Love Straw. I know." Moni waited

for some more comforting words, but none came. Her mom appeared deep in thought.

They washed the dishes together in silence.

After dinner, while they watched TV (a show where contestants competed in installing complicated light fixtures within a three-minute time limit), Raya texted the group again.

Saw you and Shim alllllll over each other at game. It's on at FNS2 tomorrow. Tati's on it.

K was all Moni texted back. Neither Harley nor Grace commented.

Chapter Twenty-One

Moni, Grace, Harley, and Raya arrived at the second Friday Night Skate of the year at 6:48 p.m. Fashionably late, fashionably in a group of four, and (not so) fashionably attired. The four girls matched in blue jeans, sky blue tank tops, and flip-flops. Sure, they looked like the ocean, a tidal wave, the sky, or teenagers at the mall ("It's sophisticated, if you think about it. More conceptual than literal," Raya explained when they'd met up to get ready). Moni felt as if she had betrayed herself by not committing to a more original or at least dynamic costume. She did note, as they entered the gym, that she didn't feel like she stood out the way she had at the first skate with Grace. Moni Hayes blended right in with the crowd.

A lot had changed since the first Friday Night Skate, Moni realized.

"Selfie!" Harley announced, holding up her phone,

empty skate floor in the background. The four girls squished together. Moni smiled dutifully, just like the others, even though she was anything but happy. Grace hadn't spoken directly to Moni since the soccer game, things were still odd with her mom, their costumes were borderline pathetic, and after Grace's explosion at the soccer game, now Johnny knew she had a crush on him, which made her feel like her skin was inside out.

There wasn't much to smile about, as far as Moni was concerned.

"I'll find Tati," Raya said once they had gotten a satisfactory photo.

"For what, again?" Moni asked. After being outed at the game, the thought of seeing, much less being near, Johnny Shim again made her very, very nervous.

"She arranges everything," Harley explained.

"Arranges what?"

"OMG, Monilee, we've been through this. What planet are you on? Wait, don't answer that," Raya said. "Now that it's basically official that you have a crush on Johnny Shim and he more than likely likes you back, Tati is going to seal the deal. Don't worry, you'll see."

Moni looked at Grace, but Grace just walked straight to the custodial closet to get her skates. If Grace told Harley and Raya about their fight, they were either playing it off well or didn't care.

"Y'all get your skates and go to the stage. I'll alert Tati and meet you there."

So Moni went and sat on the edge of the stage, letting her feet dangle. She wiggled her toes inside the clunky skates.

Surprise, surprise: Johnny was nowhere in sight. If he ever spoke to Moni again, maybe she'd get him a watch for his birthday. Or for Halloween. A watch for Halloween. Cute. That thought lightened Moni's mood a bit.

Grace wasn't giving her the time of day. She giggled with Harley, hovering next to some boys they seemed to know from soccer camp. Moni didn't catch their names, and neither Grace nor Harley introduced her. Not good manners. Alex skated by, holding out his hand for high fives. Grace was the only one who indulged him, before turning her attention back to the soccer boys. Was Grace flirting? Sure looked like it. Maybe she had a crush on one of those soccer boys, and she'd confided in Harley and not her. The thought grossed Moni out.

Moni felt like she didn't know anything anymore.

"Moni, there's your boy," Harley said, pointing to the doorway. "Or should I say, chandelier? Mop? Alien? I don't know what he is, actually."

It was him. Johnny Shim in full costumed glory. He wore what appeared to be a white shower cap on his head. Only bits of his cumulous-cloud hair peeked through underneath. Connected to the collar of his T-shirt were dozens of long strings, all of which reached past his waist. Moni couldn't tell if they were made out of ribbons, strips of fabric, or both, but they were colorful and dazzling.

Johnny Shim made a stupendous jellyfish.

"Wow," Moni whispered to herself. And then, a little louder to confirm, "Jellyfish." It was so obvious.

He looked magnificent. Despite everything, Johnny still had the ability to take her breath away. Moni automatically looked down at her necklace, even though she knew she was too far away from him for the charm to activate.

Maybe because Moni couldn't stand waiting on that stage next to Grace another second, maybe because she knew it would feel nice to skate across the floor, or maybe because she wanted to get a closer look, Moni stood with the intention of gliding directly to Johnny Shim.

But the infamous Tati intercepted before she could push off. Tati wore all black, but with a tremendous amount of glitter on her face and arms.

"I'm a biofluorescent fish. Woo the fans, scare the rivals. Duh," she said upon arrival, before Moni had the chance to ask. Tati spoke with an authority Moni had never heard from someone under the age of twenty-five. "You like Johnny Shim, right? New kid, purple shoes, wears that T-shirt all the time?"

Moni nodded. If she confirmed her feelings out loud to this sparkly stranger, she feared she'd either uncontrollably laugh or cry. No way to know which, though both, Moni predicted, would be very bad. She was starting to feel stressed. Like she had leading up to the first skate, but worse now because she didn't have Grace. Just a stupid necklace that made her feel on top of the world one moment and like scum the next. When she clutched the key-shaped charm in her hand, she felt her heart beating through her shirt. No, not beating. Pounding.

"Okay, I'll take care of it. He's the one dressed as a hanging plant?"

"Jellyfish," Moni mumbled.

"Exactly. Meet me over by the snack closet stairwell when I give you the signal."

"Got it," Raya said, answering for Moni. Moni hoped the signal would be obvious. She didn't know if she could handle making another mistake.

The signal proved to be about as subtle as Tati's body glitter.

"Moni Hayes, get over here!" Tati shouted above the music. The girl had lungs.

Raya led Moni (who was still a little shaky on her skates, as she hadn't properly warmed up) across the gym. Tati stood, as promised, right outside the door to the stairwell. Johnny Shim was next to her. The headphones boys from Mega Poppy Seed Test day lurked behind him. None of the boys wore roller skates.

Tati motioned for Moni to skate into the spot she'd made between her and Johnny. Moni obeyed.

"You guys like each other, so you're going out now. Yay."

Boy, Tati was efficient. Businesslike, even.

Now that Moni thought back on it, she sort of understood why nobody had been skating last month until the very end. She remembered the crowd around the stairwell, the announcement she couldn't hear from her spot on the bleachers. Sandwiched between Tati and Johnny Shim, facing the skate floor, she saw that most of the Friday Night Skate attendees had gathered around.

"Next stop on this train is the stairwell!" Tati proclaimed.

"Choo-choo," Raya cheered.

Friday Night Skate had so little to do with skating. Moni felt as if she'd been deceived by anyone and everyone. Was it so crazy that Moni just wanted to dress up and skate in circles and maybe hang out with Johnny Shim, but not in some strange stairwell that Tati now ushered them into?

Before the door shut behind them, Raya scurried over and whispered in her ear. "Remember, Monilcc: Not too excited, boys are babies, see you having fun! You got this!"

The door shut behind them, muffling the thumping music and the energy from their peers. They were alone, in a vacuum, it seemed.

Am I here? Moni thought to herself.

Johnny walked a few steps up the flight and took a seat on a middle stair. Moni followed behind, albeit a bit more awkwardly. Climbing stairs in roller skates was at best cumbersome, at worst hazardous.

"I guess I missed the memo, huh?" he said once Moni had taken a seat next to him. Was that too forward? Sitting a step below seemed weird, and sitting a step higher felt too similar to beating him at a competition, which she had just been reminded was a no-no.

"You look . . ." Moni had planned to say *fantastic*. Or *amazing*. Or even *perfect*. But then she remembered that those descriptors definitely indicated excitement. "Costumed," she said, carefully.

"I thought at least you would be dressed up."

"Oh," Moni said, ashamed. "I am."

"Really?"

"Yeah." Moni focused her eyes on the tip of her worn skate. "A tidal wave."

"Creative."

Moni couldn't tell if he was kidding. Sarcasm didn't seem to be a Johnny Shim thing. But then again, maybe Moni didn't yet know all there was to know about him.

"It's maybe more obvious when you see all of us together," Moni explained. She then realized how dumb that sounded. "Probably not, though."

She noticed the blue stone on her charm camouflaged into her shirt. She wished she could telepathically communicate with Grace to tell her that climbing stairs on roller skates was ridiculous. Would she ever talk to Grace again?

Moni checked her necklace again. Indigo blue, the color of her eyes.

Moni heard a new song beginning. The sound was only partially muted.

"A throwback from waaaay back," she heard DJ 10 Foot announce. A pop beat echoed through the walls. She knew this one, all the words, actually. She and Grace both did.

Moni sighed. She should be skating, arm in arm, shouting the lyrics at the top of her lungs, with Grace right now.

"What are we supposed to do in here?" Moni

asked glumly. She was having a hard time mustering a sense of fun. It was the first time she'd been alone with Johnny Shim that she wasn't utterly elated. Everything felt rotten, inside and out. The mothball smell of the stairwell certainly didn't help.

"Probably fall in love."

No, sarcasm did not suit Johnny Shim.

"Cool," Moni squeaked.

Moni checked her necklace out of habit. It was a dark, dark blue. Darker than she'd ever seen it. Not unlike the depths of the sea, actually, where jellyfish sometimes lived. It must have been the dim lighting.

"So, yeah, this is weird," Johnny mumbled.

"Pretty much the weirdest," Moni agreed. And then, "I heard a rumor that Tati is royalty in Latvia."

"Well, that explains it."

"Totally."

Moni checked her necklace. Deep blue sea.

"I'm a little distracted," Johnny Shim admitted.

"Me too," Moni said.

"Calvin and my parents got into it again."

I got into it with Grace, Moni thought.

"He thinks they're too involved with his life."

Grace thinks I only care about myself and my necklace.

Moni checked the charm. Deeper blue sea.

"He said he never wants to see any of us again."

Grace probably doesn't care if she sees me, either, because she is best friends with Harley now.

Moni checked her necklace. Deepest blue sea. Nearly black. The charm had never been that color before. Maybe it was a good sign? Probably not, but you never know. They were in stairwell territory now, you-both-officially-like-each-other territory now. Anything was possible, right?

"Are you even listening to me?"

"What?" Moni asked, blinking her way back to the present.

"Wow."

Silence ensued. Moni checked her necklace again just in case. A blue so dark it bordered on midnight.

"Why are you constantly looking at that necklace you always wear?" Johnny asked.

Moni's heartbeat accelerated.

"What do you mean?" Moni stalled.

"I always see you checking it. Do you actually think it's magic or something?" Johnny said, sounding irritated. "You know how it's annoying when you're with someone and they're, like, blatantly on their phone texting while you're talking to them?"

Boy, did she ever. Moni nodded.

"It's like that." Johnny sounded really annoyed now.

Moni didn't know what to say. She pictured Grace laughing and skating with Harley. She imagined Raya gossiping with Tati. She heard the chorus of that song: *Every morning every night, think of you and feel so right* . . . DJ 10 Foot must have turned the volume up even louder, because now Moni realized she could hear the lyrics clear as day, dark as the deep blue sea.

"Why is listening to people so hard?" Johnny asked.

But Moni didn't hear. Her ears only received the swirling thoughts in her head, and the song—the song playing through the walls that she and Grace had once recorded a lip sync video to on her first cell phone.

Call me baby, I'm right here . . .

And if there's one thing Moni Hayes hated, it was to let a song lyric go unfinished.

"Never far, always here," Moni belted absent-mindedly.

"Hah. Sure. I'm out," Johnny said, shuffling out the stairs and out the door. Moni snapped out of her daze as Johnny clambered down the stairs and out the door.

"Wait!" Moni called. She stood to go after him, to tell him that her necklace was stupid and she'd gotten in a fight with Grace, too, and she didn't know what else, but something—anything—to make it better.

But the thing with roller skates on concrete steps was that it was hard to chase. And if you tried to chase anyway, you might fall.

And that's exactly what Moni did. She tumbled. Headfirst. She managed to catch herself on the door, but the thing about doors it that they have hinges. Hinges that yielded to Moni's body, tipping her from inside the stairwell to outside, right within touching distance not of Johnny Shim (who had vanished), but Grace Diaz. And touching distance also sometimes was the same as eavesdropping distance.

Moni crashed to the floor, one body part at a time: blue jeans, sky blue tank top, Crush Necklace, heart.

Finally, the small silver key-shaped charm clanked against the ground. That's when Moni saw.

The charm wasn't dark blue. It wasn't bright blue. It wasn't any single color. Instead, it swirled and churned a fluorescent tie-dye.

The necklace had malfunctioned. Had its powers officially run out? She had to tell Grace! Maybe then everything would be okay. All her problems had started with the crazy Crush Necklace, and now that it was broken she could explain and everything between her and Grace would be okay again. Things with her and Grace had to be okay again!

As if on cue, directed by the Crush Necklace goddess herself, Grace's nearby voice floated above all other competing sounds.

"Oh yeah, Moni has a huge crush on Johnny. They're perfect for each other: Two weirdos who nobody even likes."

"Figures," Alex's voice answered.

Ping. The biggest of them all.

Moni didn't hear the rest. She pushed to her feet, ripped off her skates, and retrieved her shoes in record time. As she scrambled out the gym door—she had to get out of the Mason Mill rec center right away—she saw Grace and Alex skate onto the gym floor as a new song began. Grace looked over her shoulder, and the two girls made eye contact. Tears welled behind Moni's eyeballs. She looked away. Before she could remind herself to stifle her impulse, Moni clasped the key-shaped charm and ripped the delicate silver chain from around her neck.

Chapter twenty-two

"It broke" was all Moni managed to say as she burst through the door to her apartment before dissolving into tears. She held the wrecked chain out for her mom to see, fingers enclosing the malfunctioning charm.

"Don't worry, baby, we can get that fixed," Moni's mom said, stretching and yawning from her spot on the couch. She'd fallen asleep while doing her homework again. Despite Moni's dramatic entrance, she was still a little foggy. "Come dry off." She ushered Moni into the bathroom, where she wrapped a big towel around the shoulders of her soaking, shivering daughter.

"Not the chain. The whole thing. Everything is broken."

Once Moni started talking, she couldn't stop. She told her mom everything, starting with her purchase at Tina's Treasures a month back, to the many ways she'd tried to use the Crush Necklace to her advantage, to Raya's rules about crushes, to her suspicion that Harley liked her mom more than her, to her fight with Grace, and everything in between. Every time she thought she was done, she remembered a new detail, and another part of the story spilled out. Twenty minutes later, she had a headache and her eyes burned.

"Do you think I'm a gullible fool for believing in all that?" Moni asked, fearing the answer. "A dumb seventh grader who doesn't know any better?"

"Hey, don't speak about my Love Straw that way."

"Maybe it wasn't a magic necklace at all."

"Or maybe it was doing a different kind of magic than you realized."

"No more riddles," Moni pleaded, before tucking into bed and immediately falling into a hard, dreamless sleep.

The next morning, Moni couldn't bring herself to even think about pancakes. She lay in bed and retrieved her fun fact slash Crush Necklace journal from underneath her pillow. Reading her entries over again made her equally happy and sad. There were a lot of Johnny Shim fun facts slash Crush Necklace entries. More than she had even realized.

Fun Fact #84: Purple Converse complement a starry night mouth.

Fun Fact #85: Tiny rocks are the best for big dreams.

Fun Fact #86: You are here.

Fun Fact #87: Maybe this necklace really is made for me!

Fun Fact #88: "Boys take up a lot of space." —MH

"Only if you let them." —NH

Crush Necklace bright blue 1: Tina's Treasure's selfie ambush!

CN bright blue 2: Fingers touching post FNS Superman!

CN bright blue 3: Palomino at the mini-mart!

CN bright blue 4: Rock dream painting, tell me something good, listening with eyes and ears

CN bright blue 5: Chicken fingers without ranch are worthless

CN bright blue 6: Frisbee on snack roof till the end of time

CN bright blue 7: Poppy seed pirate

CN bright blue 8: Happy jumpy Tuesday!

CN bright blue 9: Push-ups → Popsicles please (5 less than JS)

CN bright blue 10: MMRSS victory!

CN bright blue 11: Dream rock gifting

CN bright blue 12: Cheering for Grace!

So much evidence that things were going well. What had gone wrong?

Moni shut her journal and hid it underneath her mattress. Out of sight, and hopefully soon out of mind.

That Science Sunday, Moni couldn't focus on her homework. Her energy must have been contagious, because after ten minutes her mom shut her laptop and motioned for Moni to join her on the couch.

"You know, I've been thinking about what you said the other night. About going back to sixth grade."

"Sixth grade was the best," Moni stated, though now that she'd said it again, she wasn't sure that was completely true. Yes, she'd hung out with Grace all the time, but the only other kid they really talked to was Alex, and that's because he was always annoying them. Plus, science class wasn't nearly as in depth or interesting then. And there was no Friday Night Skate yet . . . Moni's mom's voice interrupted her spiraling thoughts.

"And about the fun fact you didn't let me finish."

"Sorry."

"I'll be short and sweet: I got this tattoo because it reminds me of something that's really easy to forget, no matter how old you are."

Be yourself. Everyone else is taken. Moni read the words to herself as she gently traced the lines on her mom's soft skin.

"So you're saying we should get matching tattoos?" Moni asked, feeling the weight in her heart begin to lift.

"In your dreams," Moni's mom chided. "This is my point: Sixth grade, seventh grade, high school, dang, even an adult waitress in her second year of online college, it's still easy to forget that you at your truest is the best version of yourself. If you get in the habit of remembering that now . . ."

Moni sighed. She knew all about habits.

"It'll get easier."

"Promise?" Moni asked.

"I promise."

"That might be the most important fun fact you've ever told me," Moni admitted.

"Well, you ain't heard what Charlie told me about jellyfish during my breakfast shift this morning." Moni's mom paused for dramatic effect. "Jellyfish breathe through their skin. And their tentacles can sting even if they're disconnected from their bodies."

Moni thought about that for a minute.

"Wild, right?"

"Accurate," Moni stated.

That night, Moni dreamed she was swimming in the deep blue sea, but for some reason it wasn't all that dark or scary at all.

Perhaps out of curiosity, perhaps out of habit, when Moni woke up for school Monday morning she checked her necklace, which remained in its red velvet case on her nightstand. The charm on the Crush Necklace was black. A matte black, like a disposable spoon, or some other piece of equally unremarkable plastic. Moni noticed that the gold writing on the inside of the case had vanished, no trace in sight. When Moni unfolded the tiny paper that once contained all the Crush Necklace instructions, she nearly gasped. Instead of the sassy, personalized remarks, all that was printed on the slightly wrinkled piece of paper was a receipt:

$15

Crush Necklace

Tina's Treasures

Visit us in person, not on the web!

Moni folded up the receipt and placed it with the necklace inside the box and snapped it shut.

Moni Hayes was on her own.

Chapter twenty-three

Moni proceeded with her post–Crush Necklace life as efficiently as she could.

Twenty-four hours necklace-free, Moni still felt slightly naked without it. Like walking into preschool without a security blanket, or a stuffed animal, or the knowledge that your pet goldfish would be waiting for you when you returned home, if that was your thing. (That had been Moni's thing. RIP, Strawberry.) Moni was a little wobbly on her feet.

But also she felt a little clearer without it in a way she couldn't have predicted. At first, she still checked that dip right between her collarbones every time she happened to see Johnny Shim in the hallway or pass him on the Music Box Steps, but it didn't take too long for her to remember she was necklace-free. Some habits were easier to break than build.

Moni kept to herself at school. When she walked

between classes, she realized how much more relaxing it was to get from one place to another if you weren't under the pressure of executing some sort of Get Close to Someone Without Them Noticing Until the Last Second plan. In science class Ms. Starks transitioned to a unit on understanding plant and human cells. As going straight home after school to do homework and then to watch entertaining but bizarre non-scripted TV was getting old and science was proving to kind of be the best, Moni decided she'd sign up for chemistry club. It started the following week and was led by Ms. Starks, who was usually meaner to boys than girls as a matter of principle. Moni quite liked Ms. Starks.

Though her mind was clearer, she still hadn't spoken to Grace. She wasn't sure if she was avoiding Grace, or if Grace was avoiding her. Either way, the avoiding was executed with practiced efficacy. It had been almost five days since the last Friday Night Skate, and they had not come so close as touching distance.

Between fifth and sixth periods, as Moni was exchanging books in her locker, she felt a tap on her shoulder.

It was Raya.

"You ghosting us or something, Monilee?"

"What?"

"Full incognito mode, dude."

"Oh. I just, I dunno . . ." Her voice trailed off. "I've been thinking about stuff." Moni closed her locker and shifted the weight of her backpack to her left shoulder.

"You're in a fight with Grace."

"You know?" Moni shouldn't have been surprised, she realized.

"I'm not blind, Monilee."

"Well, I didn't think you were."

"You should talk to her. I don't know what went down, but y'all are best friends. You've got to figure it out." Moni nodded. Raya was still very good at giving instructions. "But that's not why I tracked you down. I am here to offer my humble thanks." Raya took a dramatic bow, bumping her backpack into a passerby.

"You're welcome. But for what?"

"Helping me with that science worksheet last week or whenever. Duh. Aced it, baby!" Raya shoved the paper in Moni's face. Sure enough, Ms. Starks's curly red writing read, *Better!*

"Nice!" Moni said, giving Raya a high five.

"Now I just have to master the fine art of telepathy so Ms. Starks will never give us homework again." Raya flexed her muscles, for some reason. Raya was a weirdo. One of the best kinds of weirdos, as it turned out. "Anyway, hang soon. If all goes as planned, and it rains tomorrow, soccer practice will be canceled." Before Moni could acknowledge anything she'd said, Raya bopped down the hall. "Pray for rain, pray for rain, friends," she declared into the throngs of students rushing to class.

Moni grinned and made her way to PE, a bounce in her step that had been missing since the end of sixth grade.

Coach Stoop had been out sick for a week. Something about bursting his appendix during a 2K attempt. Their sub had let them watch videos of Olympic gymnastics from the 1990s every day, which proved thrilling for basically everyone. Coach Stoop's return was not met with mixed reactions. Even Alex groaned when Coach Stoop and not their gymnastics sub walked into the gym to start class.

Moni sat in the front row of the bleachers. Ever since the second Friday Night Skate, Moni had taken to sitting in the front row of any class without assigned seats. Especially in PE, where nothing was particularly assigned, she liked for the rest of the class to be behind her. Less distracting.

"To get the elephants in the room out of the way, yes, my appendix burst, and no, you do not need your appendix to thrive."

"Duh," Alex muttered from somewhere behind her.

Moni heard a giggle. Grace. She kept her eyes on raggedy Coach Stoop.

He continued his speech. "Yes, I had to stop the marathon early—"

"I heard it was a 2K," someone in the back yelled.

"Like my grandma Mitten always said, 'There's no building block too small.'" Coach Stoop was really starting to lose it. "And no, I will not be deterred. You all can rest assured that I will be back on the track, the course, the pitch, and even the mound in no time at all."

"Yay," said an unidentifiable monotone. Moni was getting antsy. She was either ready for more gymnastics or at the very least some low-stakes dodgeball.

"That's right, ladies and gentlemen, I may be down a nonessential organ"—Coach Stoop patted his side—"but I'm back! Like my grandma Mitten always reminded me, 'Coach Stoop, don't you dare disappear—'"

"You're my dream reality!" Moni belted.

Say what you wanted about Moni Hayes, but the girl hated to let a song lyric go unfinished. Correction: Moni Hayes was incapable of letting a song lyric go unfinished.

The whole class erupted in laughter. Moni didn't know if they were laughing at her joke or at Coach Stoop, but either way it felt good. Moni heard a particularly familiar giggle. On instinct, she turned and looked over her shoulder.

Grace sat a couple rows behind her, hand over her mouth, laughing hysterically. The two girls locked eyes for a second before Moni snapped her head back forward.

"Very clever, Moni Hayes," Coach Stoop said with a grin.

Say what you wanted about Coach Stoop, but he was a good sport.

Moni rushed home after school. She hadn't looked at her fun fact slash Crush Necklace journal all week, but she was curious about something. Her moment of connection with Grace during PE gave her an idea. A hypothesis, really. A hypothesis that she just might have all the verification she needed to prove.

As Ms. Starks sometimes said, being a scientist meant using all the evidence to tell a story. And being an artist meant seeing things from all different angles. As Moni pulled her journal out from underneath her mattress, Moni planned on becoming a seventh-grade artist-scientist extraordinaire.

Without wasting the time required to flop on her bed, Moni stood in the middle of her bedroom, reading and rereading her recent entries.

The evidence was right there.

She hovered over some of the vaguer bits.

CN bright blue 8: Happy jumpy Tuesday!

She thought back to that jumpy Tuesday and tried to remember what happened. She'd made a joke. She'd scared him but also made a joke. He had laughed.

Same with *CN bright blue 9: Push-ups → Popsicles please (5 less than JS)*. She had lost the competition, or whatever, but she'd made a joke. Moni loved making jokes. It came naturally. It was her.

She backtracked to *CN bright blue 7: Poppy seed pirate*. Another joke.

The thing about jokes is, for them to work, you have to read your audience; you have to listen with your eyes and your ears.

All this explained why the gag with the pepperoni, the one-mile run, and the disastrous Mega Poppy Seed Test had failed. She hadn't been paying attention to Johnny Shim and she hadn't been acting like herself.

Her mom's tattoo came to mind. *Be yourself. Everyone else is taken.*

Moni closed her eyes and did her best to remember each and every scenario. Not just what happened but how she felt. She began to notice a pattern. An undeniable pattern.

Was it possible that Moni had been interpreting the bright blue on her Crush Necklace incorrectly this whole time? Moni was immediately able to answer her own question. Maybe the Crush Necklace not only indicated when Moni's crush was feeling her, but indicated when Moni Hayes was being the most true version of Moni Hayes. Maybe Johnny Shim crushed hardest on Moni Hayes when she was her 100 percent, unfiltered self.

Without hesitation, Moni picked up her phone and texted Grace.

Meet me at TTs after practice. 5 p.m. Emergency. Please. Then, I love you and I miss you.

Moni remembered something Raya had said to her way back on that walk to the first Friday Night Skate. *Don't tell him you like him.* What strange advice. If you love someone, or like someone, or think they have cool hair and a very interesting brain, what was wrong with letting them know?

Same went for your best friend.

Chapter twenty-four

Moni sat on the curb outside of Tina's Treasures. She'd gotten there twenty minutes early because she could no longer stand pacing inside her apartment. Roxanna had already been outside twice to remind Moni that loitering was an unbecoming quality. Whatever that meant.

Roxanna was still, well, Roxanna.

Moni hugged her knees to her chest. The red velvet box inside her hoodie pocket pressed against her thigh. Moni resisted the urge to check her cell phone. The volume was on. She'd hear if anyone tried to contact her. Soccer practice ended at 4:30. Grace should be arriving any minute. If she was going to come at all; Moni received no text back. Deep down, Moni's intuition told her Grace would show.

Moni was right. Grace strolled up at 5:07. Fashionably late.

"Yo," she said with a little wave. She sat on the curb next to Moni.

"Hi."

The both took deep breaths.

"Okay, I'll start," Grace said.

"No, me," Moni interjected.

"Okay."

"I'm sorry I've been a bad friend. I got carried away with the Crush Necklace stuff, and that was stupid. But I miss you and I'm sorry and I want things to go back to normal."

Grace kicked a rock.

"And . . ." Moni took another breath for courage. This was the hardest part to admit. "I felt really weird, and I guess jealous, when you came back from camp and had all these new friends. And I realized something about this Crush Necklace, too. It didn't help me read Johnny Shim's mind. Not at all. It told me when I was being myself. Unfortunately, it didn't teach me how to listen."

"Deep," Grace said after a few beats.

Deep blue sea, Moni thought to herself.

"At first the necklace made me feel less crazy about my stupid crush. But then I guess it made me crazy in a different way," Moni admitted. "Anyway, it's broken now. The magic is gone, or whatever."

"They do call it a crush for a reason," Grace said finally. "Raya told me that."

"Of course she did."

"Duh."

"Duh."

The girls sat in silence. A few brittle leaves blew across the otherwise empty parking lot.

"Okay, where do I start?" Grace asked. "I'm really sorry. Like really, really sorry. I should never have said that stuff at the soccer game and at the skate. I was just so mad. It's like you disappeared!"

"Yeah," Moni said.

"Life without you sucks. You're my literal favorite. Fa-vo-rite," Grace emphasized, breaking the word into syllables. "I can't have my best friend disappear!"

Grace admitted that maybe she got a little carried away trying to impress Harley and Raya when she got back from soccer camp. And Moni confessed that the soccer crowd was intimidating at first, but in truth, they were great. It was fun to have more friends, they both agreed. Soon, the tension between them began to evaporate.

"Anyway, I guess I should spill it. You're not the only one with a crush these days," Grace revealed coyly.

"A soccer camp boy? One of Much Love's friends?" Moni guessed.

Grace shook her head, blushed, and covered her eyes with her hands. "You're never going to let me live this down: Alex!"

"No!" Moni exclaimed.

"It's true! I don't know what happened, but something must have changed over the summer and it's like he's not the annoying Alex he always was."

"He's the cute Alex that sweeps you off your feet?"

"Basically," Grace admitted. "And I guess now that I think about it, I felt a little jealous, or left out, or like a baby or something when you had this big old crush and I didn't. You were getting all this attention and being so proactive about it—I mean, you literally got a magic necklace—and I felt like I was just behind or something."

Wow. Moni never would have guessed.

"But now you've found Alex. Swoon city."

"Swoondom, more like it. And trust me, no necklace required. That boy is a flirrrrt." Grace giggled.

"And nice and cute and I don't even mind his braces or applesauce smell anymore—what is wrong with me, Moni?!"

Moni laughed and threw her arm around her best friend. "Absolutely nothing. Crushes are very confusing." It felt good to say the truth. "And sometimes the worst," Moni added.

"Slash best."

"Best slash worst."

"Best slash worst," they agreed.

Wow. Seventh grade was weird. And confusing. Weird slash confusing. Best slash sometimes the worst. But maybe it was all going to be okay.

"Absolutely not," Roxanna said, refusing to even touch the red box. "No returns, no exchanges, no actual thrifting on premises. What is so hard about that to understand?" she asked, pointing to the handwritten sign taped to the register. The tape around the edges of the light pink paper was peeling.

"No, we're gifting it," Moni insisted.

"That's different," Grace clarified. "A gift is—"

"I know what a gift is, I played an elf in the

Christmas pageant last year, thank-you-very-much." Moni and Grace looked at each other and stifled a giggle. Roxanna was full of surprises. "No gifting, either. You can throw it in the garbage or *gift* it to one of your third grade—"

"Seventh grade!" Moni and Grace interrupted together.

"Whatever. Y'all get out of here before I call Tina. Love you, don't mean it, bye."

Roxanna shooed the girls out the door, back into the parking lot.

"I don't think it's right to actually throw it in the garbage," Moni said as she paced back and forth, considering their options. They'd continued to loiter for five minutes after being kicked out of the store, and Moni had a feeling Roxanna was going to yell at them any minute if they didn't get a move on. Despite all the trouble that ensued, Moni felt very fondly toward her Crush Necklace. Correction: her retired Crush Necklace. Her gut told her it didn't belong to her anymore.

"Def not," Grace said, kicking a rock.

"You want it? The silver key will really make the shine on Alex's braces pop," Moni teased.

"Don't even," Grace said, kicking a bigger rock across the lot.

That gave Moni an idea. A possibly brilliant one.

"Follow me," she said. A statement, not a question.

Thirty minutes and a pit stop at the mini-mart for mini marshmallows and cherry Cokes later, Moni and Grace found themselves on the slightly blustery shore of Bell Lake.

"You were great while you lasted," Moni said, kissing the black stone on the key-shaped charm. She placed the broken silver chain on the red satin bed inside the red velvet gold-writing-less box and snapped the case closed. It made a satisfying *pop*. "What if it washes up on the shore?" Moni asked.

"Nah, the current will take it away."

"Not sure lakes have currents, Grace."

"Well, this one has motorboats and there's all this wind," Grace said, gesturing to the air around them. "You know what I mean."

"I do," Moni said, because she did.

"On the count of three. One . . . two . . . three!"

Moni wound up, then hurled the Crush Necklace,

box and all, into Bell Lake. The momentum of the throw catapulted her forward. Managing to catch herself before the nosedive was complete, Moni spotted something on the dirt-sand right by her foot.

She picked up a flat piece of slate, no bigger and no smaller than a peanut butter cup, and slid it in her pocket.

Like it or not, Moni Hayes still had a crush on Johnny Shim.

Chapter twenty-five

With things back on track with Grace, Moni was in an extra-good mood the next day. The commencement of chemistry club was just icing on the cake. Or the pecans on monster pie. Same thing.

"I know y'all thought we were doing chemistry, but we're going to start with astronomy," Ms. Starks said as she whooshed into room 201, the dedicated meeting place for chemistry club.

"Like Gemini/Leo/Taurus astronomy?" the girl with the chipped nail polish asked. Her name was Sage. Today she worked on removing a leftover speck of magenta from her pointer finger. "Is that what you're talking about?"

"Libra season, baby!" Alex yelled. He really was everywhere. Especially when there was extra credit involved.

"Alex, calm yourself. And no, not at all what I'm talking about. Anyone in here who spends less than ten hours on the internet a day want to tell me the difference between astrology and astronomy?"

Moni raised her hand high. "The difference is . . ." Her voice trailed off.

Johnny Shim, the same Johnny Shim who she hadn't spoken to since the stairwell of that awful Friday Night Skate, who still wore his purple Converse, whose hair looked like a cumulous cloud, walked through the door and into room 201.

"So nice of you to join us," Ms. Starks said.

"Sorry I'm late," he said, adjusting his backpack. "Chemistry club?"

"The one and only. Pick a seat, any seat."

Moni watched Johnny Shim look around the room. There was a seat next to Alex, Sage, and on either side of those two boys currently not wearing their headphones. And next to her.

Without hesitation, Johnny walked to the open spot next to Moni and sat down. Her stomach tingled, and she wiggled her toes underneath the table.

After Moni successfully explained the difference

between astronomy and astrology, Ms. Starks told them that day one was for science-art. She distributed crayons, paper, rulers, erasers, markers, glue sticks, Sharpies, and feathers (of all things).

"Make an image of something true about yourself or your universe. Conceptual is fine. Literal works. Do your thing," she instructed. "Anyone who behaves will get glitter. Look at me talking like y'all are a bunch of toddlers. Do your work. Don't throw pencils. Be right back."

Ms. Starks walked out the door, presumably to get a cup of coffee from the teachers' lounge.

This was not at all what Moni had expected chemistry club to be, but she didn't mind. Sometimes things turned out better than expected. Plus, Moni Hayes was no novice science-artist.

She had an idea. Go time.

Moni and the other members of the fledgling chemistry club picked out their art supplies of choice. She didn't need feathers or crayons or erasers or glue, Moni realized. Just a permanent marker.

Moni reached into the small pocket of her backpack and felt for the baggie that she knew was still there. She took out a single Popsicle stick, uncapped the red Sharpie in her hand, and wrote in block letters, without hesitation or pause, not second-guessing her impulse once.

When she was finished, and without any explanation, she handed the Popsicle stick to Johnny. His fingers clasped the other end. Moni hesitated to let go. For just a moment, they both held on together.

Moni looked at the block letters written neatly on the electric blue–stained stick. She watched Johnny Shim move his lips while he read her writing, though no sound came out. That's probably what she looked like when she counted his freckles, Moni realized.

What she would have also written on the Popsicle stick if it could fit was this: *Johnny Shim, I think you're great but very confusing, and I love your rocks and your shoes and your hair, and I think you need to practice running because you are very slow, but overall you're great, and this Popsicle stick was made for you and your dreams.*

She hoped the three words that fit conveyed all that. She thought they might.

"*We are here,*" Johnny Shim read from the stick in

a whisper so quiet only Moni could hear. And then, "You are awesome, Moni Hayes."

Moni smiled and looked him in the eye.

I am, she thought.

"Thanks."

Chapter Twenty-Six

So things went back to how they'd always been pre–Crush Necklace. Except not really. Everything was the same and everything was different.

Now that it was too chilly to go to Bell Lake on the weekends, Moni sometimes joined Harley, Raya, Grace, and some soccer camp boys for bowling or burgers. Moni finally learned how to kick a soccer ball using the inside of her foot, so there were no more big-toe casualties. The soccer boys were a lot at first but soon proved harmless. Much Love was afraid of bumblebees but also gave great hugs. Easy turned out to be really good at dancing and was teaching Moni how to do that move where you jumped down into a split and then stood up. BG laughed at most of Moni's jokes.

Harley and Moni finally stopped feeling so threatened by the other (Harley had felt intimidated by

Moni since day one!). They discovered that they shared a passion for outdated video games (courtesy of Moni's mom and Harley's video-game-obsessed twin brothers) and writing in their respective journals. Raya remained bossy and boy crazy and hilarious, her prayers for rain answered a whopping 50 percent of the time.

Moni and Grace still went to Tina's Treasures, just the two of them. Sometimes before a Friday Night Skate, sometimes on a random Saturday after pancakes or if soccer practice was canceled. The next soccer game, Grace started at right wing and played the entire time, scoring not one but two goals. Moni cheered until her voice was hoarse.

Moni and her mom still shared fun facts every day. Sometimes Moni's were about Johnny Shim, but just as often they described what she'd learned in science class, a new sound she'd heard, or a surprising sight she'd seen on her way home from school. Moni was getting really good at listening with her ears and her eyes.

Moni and Johnny Shim got together to paint. Sometimes at the lake, even though it was getting chilly, sometimes at her apartment. Sometimes after watching Grace, Harley, and Raya's soccer game. On November 11, Moni kissed him on the cheek after he showed her a particularly conceptual dream-rock painting. She couldn't resist. He blushed and then kissed her back, on the lips. Afterward, Moni wiggled her toes and smiled. She told Grace about it, but nobody else.

Moni thought about the Crush Necklace sometimes. Not all the time, but sometimes. Like Moni's mom felt when she looked at her tattoo, the memory of the Crush Necklace proved a great reminder for Moni Hayes.

Pretty soon, seventh grade was halfway over, and the first Friday Night Skate after winter recess approached. The theme was Sweet Tooth. Moni had an emergency chemistry club meeting after school, so the girls planned to pick her up at her apartment on the way. The afternoon before, Grace and Moni picked up supplies for four group costumes at Tina's. When Moni presented the lewks she'd fashioned for their crew at lunch, Harley and even Raya were speechless. Moni created costumes representing each of their favorite sweets: candy corn for Harley, Swedish Fish for Raya, and matching mini marshmallows, made of strewn-together pillowcases and way too many cotton balls, for Moni and Grace. Duh.

"Girls are here," Moni's mom called from the front door. "If you don't get your tail out here, I'm gonna let Harley design my next tattoo!"

"Really?" Moni heard Harley exclaim.

"In your dreams, baby girl."

"One sec!" Moni said. Chemistry club had run late, but that wasn't why she wasn't already outside waiting for her friends. She sat on her bed, fun fact journal open to the last page on her lap. There was only room for one more entry.

Moni could hear the faint sounds of her girls laughing outside. Raya was probably arranging them in the perfect poses for selfie after selfie. Moni couldn't wait to skate with Johnny Shim. They'd arrived at the dance fashionably late, sometime after 6:30 but definitely before 7:00. He had a mega costume planned, but wanted to keep it a surprise.

"Ramona Dylan Hayes," Grace said, appearing in her bedroom doorway. "You are my fav-o-rite, but you need to hurry your butt up. We can't start taking group photos till you get out here, and you know I'm going to need at least eight hundred before we go."

"You look great," Moni said, admiring her handiwork.

"We look great. Now come on," Grace insisted.

Moni smiled at her best friend. "Okay."

Without another thought, Moni scribbled fun fact #136 in her journal, leaving the book open for any and all to see.

You are here, Moni Hayes. You are right here.

About the Author

Jessie Paddock holds a BFA in Drama from NYU's Tisch School of the Arts and an MFA in writing for children from the New School. She has lived in New York City for a while now, although she sometimes misses her hometown of Atlanta. She loves to play soccer and ride her bike to places she's never been. This is her second novel.